HOWL
Monster Boyfriends

MEG ALIVIEN

Duke Books

HOWL

Meg Alivien

Published by Duke Books

Edited by Kelly Hammond (Pickles Editing)

Cover Design by Maria Spada

Front Interior Art by irdeinfierno

Illustrations & Chapter Headers by Olivia Eaton

Print ISBN: 979-8-9878134-4-7

Ebook: 979-8-9878134-5-4

Printed in USA

HOWL

MEG ALIVIEN

Duke Books

Content Warnings

This novel contains three explicit sex scenes, detailed depictions of anxiety / panic attacks, physical & mental abuse by an ex-boyfriend, a dark humor joke about self-harm, foul language, mentions of blood, and a strained mother/daughter relationship.

There is also a scene in which a man threatens the FMC at a crowded outdoor event. Given the current climate in the U.S., I understand that this scene might bring up serious triggers for some readers. If any of these warnings make you uncomfortable, please consider protecting your mental health before proceeding.

For me,
because I needed this one.

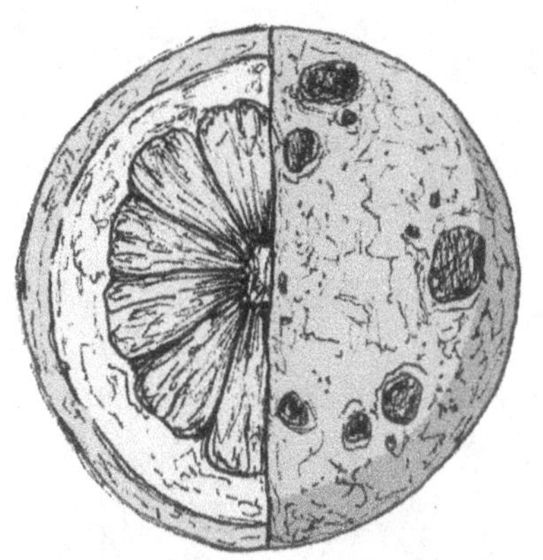

PART ONE:

Waxing

Chapter One

RAEGAN

’m lost in the pages of a brand new romance novel when I hear the faint sound of my name being called. I can’t bring myself to look up until I’ve finished reading one more paragraph. I eagerly flip the page and sigh when I see the two main characters have just accidentally grabbed for the same cup of coffee.

I’m swooning at the coincidence when I hear my name again, slightly louder this time.

“Miss Baker.”

I blink, clearing my dazed vision and find the affronted stare of Bound and Buried Bookshop’s surly manager.

“I’m sorry, Ethan,” I apologize quickly, hastily hiding the book behind my back. “What did you say?”

He clears his throat, not hiding his annoyance. “Your shift, Miss Baker, does not end for another fifteen minutes.”

“Sorry, Ethan.” I apologize again, even though I view reading this book as an important part of my job.

As much as I’ve tried to explain to him that I like to peruse the new additions as they come in, he refuses to see it as anything but loitering. I tried to explain reading new inventory would help with recommendations for customers, which would mean more business, but he didn't agree. No shock there.

The first month I worked at Bound and Buried, I started making little piles of books to buy. I found so many interesting ones I'd never heard of, and even some old favorites with covers I'd never seen. Then came Ethan, saying I needed to save them for the "real" customers, which apparently I was not. Joke's on him, since I buy them the second my shift is over, with or without his approval. Luckily for him, I'm not in the mood to debate today, so with my best ass-kissing grin, I place the book back on the shelf where it belongs.

Once his back is turned, I quickly pull up my audiobook app and smirk to myself while I add the title to my wishlist. Unfortunately, my win is short lived as a new phone call interrupts my screen. The name triggers an instant reflex to ignore it, possibly even toss it in the trash. I hit my phone's screen and send the caller to voicemail with so much force it sends a throb through my finger. *Good. Something else to focus on.*

I make my way through the crowded wooden bookshelves and push the missed phone call to the back of my mind. It's the tenth I've ignored since my shift started eight hours ago, and I refuse to break. Good thing I'm in one of my favorite places— the cozy stay-a-while vibes of Shadow Hills' one and only book store can always bring me out of a sour mood.

I spend my last fifteen minutes straightening up behind the checkout counter, tossing any stray receipts and straightening the brown paper shopping bags. Then, when the digital clock on the register reads 4:00 P.M., I grab my things from the back office and head outside to my car.

I wave to Ethan as I leave, a perfect-employee grin plastered on my face. He shoots me back that special scowl I know means "Have a great evening!" A man of few words, my boss.

Once the door shuts behind me, I breath in the fresh fall air and look around. Main Street is lined with the essential businesses of any small town: a pharmacy stocked with limited essentials, a twenty-four hour movie theater that wafts the smell of freshly popped buttery popcorn no matter what time of day and is constantly playing the same film from 1985 on repeat because the owner is in their Brat Pack era, the bookstore uncoincidentally placed next door to my best friend Jamie's sophisticated coffee shop, and even an ice cream parlor featuring different spooky flavors every week (this week is Bloody Mary, a blood orange sorbet topped with globs of raspberry syrup).

Shadow Hills is the precise vision that comes to mind when picturing a small town. Cobblestone streets wind through aged buildings, and there are year-round pumpkins in all the windows. Though it's well known for its supernatural tourism draw, for me Shadow Hills is just home. It was built one hundred and nineteen years ago and was meant to seclude, but also provide for, Tennessee's paranormal residents.

I spot Kendra, a petite and curvy banshee with cropped red hair, walking with her black cat, Scooter, and give her a wave. Trailing behind them is a line of six kittens, born only six weeks ago. The mother, Daisy May, is a tortoise shell, so the mix of warm colors on each kitten is unique. My heart fills with joy at the sight of their tiny tails and precious paws—a little family on their daily stroll—and I have to remind myself that my cat, Cleetus, does not want any brothers or sisters right now. He's a spoiled white and gray short hair, and I love him like he's my only child.

She catches my greeting from the corner of her eye and returns the gesture with a bright smile, but with her focus off the sidewalk in front of her, she accidentally runs into Woody Deadmane, an older werewolf with a severe cat allergy. He lets out an obnoxious sneeze the moment he makes contact with Kendra's sweater, and I can't help but giggle. But when her gasp of surprise turns into a screech, I have to cover my ears.

Though I'm human, I've lived among paranormals my entire life. My family is full of witches, but somehow that gene chose to skip me. I might not have magic, but I've never felt envious of my other family members. So far, I've preferred walking through life as a human. In this town, we tend to fade into the background, and that's the precise place I like to be.

Unfortunately, the one person I can't seem to hide from is Mavis Bleaker. I eye her headed my way as I near my car, trying to move as quickly as possible without drawing her attention. She's wearing a layered purple dress made from what looks like gauze material, no doubt one of Genevra's dresses, or as Mavis refers to her: Great-Gama Ginny. *Cue an eye roll.* Genevra is the current head of the Shadow Hills coven, but has been on her death bed for the past several months. It's been hard on the witches, watching their elder pass so slowly, but when the time does come, my grandmother, Moira, will take her place as leader, as she is the second eldest in the coven.

Though the circumstances are bleak, they haven't stopped Mavis from raiding Genevra's closet. Like me, her family's magic did not choose her, but Mavis will do anything she can to stand out. She insists that one day her time will come. In fact, she already claims to have the ability of sight, though the majority of her information comes from town gossip.

I wait by my car, one hand on the door handle, so close to my escape, as she waves me down, her bell sleeves blowing in the October breeze.

"I had a feeling you'd be here!" Mavis cheers, her full grin on display.

I roll my eyes and mutter, "Because I work here." Though I'm sure she 'saw' me coming.

"Oh dear, whatever's the matter?" she asks as she approaches, her smile falling.

"Nothing," I say, eyebrows scrunching, a bit confused. "Why?"

"Well, you look a bit ragged," she says earnestly.

This is the second time today I've had to swallow a salty retort, but I can't hide the purse of my lips. "Just me with no makeup, Mavis."

I open the car door and drop my bag inside, but she places a bony hand on the frame. "Is there something you need?" I ask, looking down at her perfectly manicured and sparkly red nails before meeting her gaze, trying to mask my irked tone.

"Well, yes," she admits. "I'm checking in to see if you'll be renewing your lease again at the end of the month. I have a few applicants on my waitlist, and I'd like to give them a definite answer soon."

Of course. Mavis owns the apartment building where I'm currently renting a single bedroom unit. If this town weren't so small, I could have found a better option by now, maybe further from town and more suited to my price range. The apartment complex is only a block over from the fire station, and its proximity to Main Street gives Mavis the ability to jack up the price for room and board.

"Can I get back to you on that?" I slip inside the car and sit in the driver's seat. I hate being rude, but this woman is crowding the hell out of my personal bubble.

"I've tried reaching you, dear, but you're always working." *Yeah, so I can afford your rent.*

"I'll give you an answer by the end of the month," I promise, then I buckle my seatbelt and give her a little wave.

With a tilt of her head and a gentle sigh, she releases my door and steps back onto the sidewalk. I reach out and shut the door before she can change her mind. And then, just like clockwork, I hear the muffled buzzing of my phone coming from inside my purse.

I groan and pull my sweaty hair from my neck to twist it into a bun. I've officially reached my breaking point, but as much as I want to turn off my phone all together, my anxiety reminds me there could be an emergency.

So instead, I take a deep breath and answer it. "Hey babe."

"Where the fuck have you been?" Patrick demands.

"I've been at work. I told you I had to open the store this morning." I keep my voice light and innocent. "Ethan had another dentist appointment," I say with a chuckle. "He may be a tightass, but he's got perfect teeth."

Patrick ignores my attempt at humor and holds tight to his anger, despite me never knowing what I've done wrong. "You didn't answer last night either."

"Sorry. I went to sleep early." I can't help the agitation that sneaks into my voice. I'm so sick of apologizing to someone I've known for three and a half weeks. After dodging incessant calls for days, I decide I have officially had enough. What I've been putting off for a week needs to happen tonight. "I was hoping we could get dinner tonight," I suggest, casually. "Let's go to Bones."

"I don't want to go out. Come to my place," he commands.

I hesitate, knowing that's probably not the safest idea, but relent anyway.

"Okay, sure."

I would rather break up with him in a public place, given I don't know how he's going to react, but maybe I can just hover by the door and rip off the bandaid.

Jamie will not be happy about this.

"I need to run a few errands, but I'll be there around six."

He starts to ask what my errands are, but I fein an interruption and cut the call short. "Sorry, someone needs help crossing the road. See you tonight."

I hang up the phone before Patrick can add an offensive retort. How did I end up with such a keeper? My dating life has never been the best, but if this is the type of man I'm working with, I've officially hit the bottom of the dating pool.

After my encounter with Mavis, and now the phone call with Patrick, there's no way I'm going home, so instead I head for the next best thing.

Chapter Two

JAMIE

I despise cleaning the dishes.

Yes, I own a dishwasher. I just don't use it. The same broken unit that came with the house is currently being used as a fancy drying rack.

The current state of my kitchen is clear evidence that I am great at procrastinating. I try to clean as I use things—a fork and plate here, a skillet and spatula there—but one moment of thinking, "I'll clean it in the morning" leads to days of piled up dishes. Now here I am, thirty minutes into scrubbing and I'm only halfway done.

I listen to a sports podcast to pass the time. Typically, I have the volume turned up past the doctor recommended limit so I don't hear how much water I'm wasting by leaving the faucet running. That's probably why I don't hear the front door open. And it's most definitely why, when I feel a tap on my shoulder, my immediate reflex is to pick up a knife and brandish it like a sword.

Instead of a robber, or a disorderly neighbor entering my condo uninvited, it's my best friend, Raegan. Her freckled cherub face is adorably scrunched into a look of panic, and when I glance down to see what she's so upset about, I see her arm is bleeding.

"Oh shit!" I gasp, dropping the knife. "I'm so sorry!"

I clutch her arm, fingers sliding over her soft skin, and try to staunch the flow of blood, but in reality, I'm just smearing it everywhere.

"Ow, Jamie! Get a rag or something!"

Right. Probably should've done that in the first place.

I yank a hand towel from its rack to press it to her cut, but Raegan shrieks and yanks her arm back. "You're not using that dirty thing on my open wound! I could get gangrene!"

I grab a clean one from the sink instead. "Raegan, I am so sorry. I didn't hear you come in."

She's not crying, something I take as a good sign, but she's definitely concerned. Though the gangrene comment might have come out as a joke, knowing the way her brain works, she's most likely considering the likelihood of that actually happening.

"Are you auditioning as a scream queen or something?" she jabs. "Shouldn't you be used to me coming over unannounced by now?"

"I was distracted. Hold this." I place her delicate hand over the towel and dart for the half-bath where I keep my first aid kit to retrieve bandages and antiseptic. When I return to Raegan's side, the bleeding has mostly stopped, so I'll be able to clean and cover the wound easily.

She winces again at the sting from the antiseptic, and though I know it will help, I hate seeing her in pain. I carefully place a pink bubblegum themed bandaid over the cut and when I glance up to check her expression, she's smiling.

"Where'd that come from?" she teases in a sing-song voice.

"I'm pretty sure it's been in this box since my sister was a toddler."

She grimaces at the bandaid like it's my dirty kitchen towel. "Will it work?"

I snort. "It's a bandaid, Rae. Not a condom."

This makes her freckled cheeks go pink. Raegan has never been one to openly talk about sex. For some reason, it embarrasses her, especially with me. Which is a fact I love to exploit.

She quickly changes the subject. "What's got you so jumpy?"

Her ability to see past my mishap to whatever is bubbling underneath just proves she knows me as well as I know her.

I've felt extremely on edge lately—like I've been waiting for the next shoe to drop, or for an inconvenience the size of a natural disaster to hit unexpectedly. Everything around me has just felt a little off kilter, and I know exactly why.

Unfortunately, I can't tell her.

So instead, I say, "I was fully zeroed in to this podcast I'm listening to. You know how I get about football."

Raegan narrows her eyes and smirks. She doesn't believe me, but she doesn't ask any further questions.

"Besides," I add, crouching beside her, "you always text me."

"I know, I'm sorry." She rolls her eyes and frowns. "Mavis stopped me as I was leaving work, so I drove straight here to escape her."

Understanding washes over me. "Is she asking about your lease again?"

Raegan nods. "You know I hate it there, and if I could move somewhere more affordable, I totally would, but there's just nothing available right now."

She's right—I know exactly how much she's struggled to keep up with Mavis's exorbitant price hikes. I've offered for her to move in with me many times, but each offer has been rejected. Raegan tends to refuse help from others given she would feel overwhelmed with the need to repay the kindness, though I've told her it isn't necessary with me.

I already know what her response will be, but I extend the offer one more time. "And I have the perfect solution to that problem."

She narrows her eyes, but she knows I'm right.

For the past ten years, I've been lucky to have a fully-paid, two-story condo gifted to me by my parents. I was sixteen when we moved to Shadow Hills. It was a necessary move, according to my parents, that would promise me the best life. But after allowing me the time to grow up in a place that accepted me for who I am, my parents missed their community and their friends. Once I was a legal adult, they gave me the choice to go back to Nashville with them, or stay here and begin my own life. I chose the latter. Now it's just me and two empty bedrooms.

"Come on," I insist. "I'd love to have you as a roommate. I have all this space and no one to share it with."

I see the tension in her shoulders relax, but her face conveys a different feeling.

"Jamie, I've already told you, I can't accept something like that. I'm not going to live in your condo rent-free."

"Fine, I'll charge you rent. One dollar a day."

She playfully slaps my arm but winces as the movement strains her new injury.

I place a gentle hand over the bandage and look up at her thick black lashes framing her bright blue eyes. "Seriously, Rae. What is so wrong with me offering you a hand? It's not a big deal. You stay here for as long as you need to build up your savings, then you can look for the place of your dreams."

She doesn't give me an answer to my question, so instead I say, "Just think about it, okay?"

She nods her head, and I'm shocked she's actually considering.

"Deal." I return to my feet and begin cleaning drops of blood off the linoleum.

Raegan goes to the refrigerator and grabs a fancy prebiotic soda that I only buy for her. She pops open the tab and takes a long sip, then she sits back down.

I toss the dirty paper towel into the trash and join her at the kitchen table. "How was the opening shift?" I ask, knowing she typically closes at the bookstore during the week.

"Slow," she answers. "No one recreationally shops that early. Frivolous spending tends to happen after the sun goes down."

I snort. "And why do you think that is?"

"The best bad decisions are always made after dark."

"Buying a book is a bad decision?"

"If you're like me it is. I was able to hide four new books I want behind a stack of *Guns Digest* this morning, and I already know there's no more room on my shelves to put them."

This time I let out a true laugh. "*Guns Digest?*"

"Ethan will never find them. Not his demographic."

My laughter seems to be contagious as Raegan giggles in between sips of her orange cream soda.

"Do you have plans tonight?" I ask, a residual smile still on my face after thinking about Ethan reading a gun magazine. "Wanna do our Friday night movie ritual? The theater is still playing *The Breakfast Club*, but we can watch something here."

One of our favorite things to do is watch movies together. During this time of year, when the weather starts to cool and the leaves turn stunning shades of yellow and orange, we love to watch over-the-top horror movies, the more fake blood the better.

"I can't. I'm going to break up with Patrick."

My hackles immediately stand in alert. "Shit. You're finally going to do it?"

Raegan shrugs as if it isn't a big deal, but I've been dreading this for a month.

From the moment she started dating Patrick, I knew the guy was bad news. He is way too clingy, and not in an insecure kinda way. He's possessive of her to the point that she can't schedule anything with me before confirming with him first. They've only been dating for a few weeks, and somehow he's already hooked his creepy little claws into her, treating her as if she solely belongs to him. Not to mention he's disrespectful as hell.

Thankfully, Raegan is smart when it comes to detecting bullshit. She saw the red flags after the third date, but the guy's scary personality has made it a bit difficult for her to bring up the 'things-aren't-working-out' conversation. I'm all for double-teaming the prick and going with her to finish the job, but she insists it'll be fine.

"It's time," she tells me. "My phone hasn't stopped ringing for two days."

"Where are you going to do it? You know Maurice won't mind a public disturbance at Bones. You'll serve as the evening entertainment."

Raegan bites her lip and her shoulders raise to her ears.

"What?"

"I may have agreed to go to his house."

"Absolutely not."

"Jamie–"

"No. You know that's a bad idea. I don't trust the guy as far as I can throw him, and it's not far, Rae."

She hides her smirk beneath her hand. That's definitely not true. I could probably toss him across a football field, but she doesn't need to know that.

Suddenly, she lowers her forehead to the table and lightly bangs her head against the surface in defeat, the sound ricocheting through the open kitchen. I know she wouldn't actually hurt herself, but I still slide my palm between her forehead and the next impending hit.

I hear her mumble against the table. "My life is falling apart."

"It's not," I insist. "Just let me go with you."

She lifts her head suddenly and shoots her hand out to grab my arm. "Please don't. It will only make him more angry."

"Fuck him," I snap back resolutely. "I don't care what emotion I make him feel. I'm coming. It's not safe for you to go by yourself."

Raegan eventually relents with a sigh. "Ok just...stay in the car."

Chapter Three

RAEGAN

A few hours later, I'm riding through the center of town with Jamie in his light blue pickup. The string lights that line the buildings along main street are just beginning to flicker on as the sun sets. I see Maurice opening the awning at Bones and setting up the outside tables for tonight's performance. Every weekend he features a different local artist. Turns out Shadow Hills has a lot of singer-songwriters. Jamie and I were there for dinner a few weeks ago, and we saw a really talented young ghost playing guitar and singing about the boy she liked when she was alive. Jamie chuckled when I got misty eyed over the moving performance but still slung his arm around my shoulder.

Every building we pass has been decorated to the nines for the Halloween season. Everyone displays little hints of Halloween throughout the year, but our Founding Day Festival is the biggest tourist draw. On October 30th, tourists flock to Shadow Hills to experience the ambiance of a spooky small town. Orange and yellow foliage wraps every street light, sign, and railing in sight. There are pumpkins at every doorstep, stacks of hay strategically placed on every street corner, and each business leans into their own theme. Kiki's Cafe is my favorite. It's the most popular spot to eat in town, and right now it's covered in fake cobwebs and cut out bats stuck to every square inch of the windows.

As we make our way through the roundabout in the center of town, I take in the slowly changing leaves that fall sporadically between the buildings. Shadow Hills truly is beautiful in the fall. It's the season that makes our small town charm truly shine.

We continue on past the pharmacy, behind the strip mall, and take the back road to my apartment complex. Because yes, I live in the same complex as Patrick, luckily in opposite buildings. We actually met when the dryer in my building was broken and I had to take a basket of sopping wet clothes over to his instead. The flirting had felt straight out of a romcom. He knew all the right words to say to sweep me off my feet, and for a casual relationship, the convenience worked well.

For a while.

I think the first time I knew something was wrong was when he lost it on my cat, Cleetus. Patrick had been sitting on my couch, casually sipping on a hard cider when Cleetus jumped into his lap. As Cleetus's mother, I know he's just overly friendly and wanted to introduce himself to a new person. Unfortunately, this caused Patrick to spill his drink and trigger what little patience I wasn't aware he had to get lost in a hissy fit. He jumped to his feet, sending Cleetus flying across the room, and started screaming at him for being a dumb animal.

He later apologized, of course, but from that moment I started thinking of a way to tell him this wasn't going to work. I mean, who curses out a cat? *What a douche.*

Jamie pulls in and parks a few spots away from the stairwell that leads to Patrick's second floor apartment.

I open the passenger door and hop out. "Remember," I tell him, "stay in the truck."

He rolls his eyes and scowls, and I know very well that's not going to happen. To be honest, it makes me feel safer knowing Jamie is here if something does go wrong.

Jamie has always been a safe place for me. I've known him since he was the new kid at Shadow Hills High School his senior year. I was a sophomore with no friends and no social life, but I certainly acted like I ran the place. Truthfully, we probably would have never met if I hadn't been the one assigned to show him around on his first day. Because of my good grades, I was allowed to work in the office as a student assistant for one hour a day. Most of the time it was boring, filing papers and keeping record of student attendance, but that day was one I'll always remember.

I'd just turned sixteen with braces on my teeth and fresh-cut bangs that were too short for my forehead, and there was this beautiful older boy standing in front of me. He had a quirky smile with naturally straight teeth, dirty blond hair that curled around his ears, and a presence that made you want to look at him when he entered a room. I was immediately infatuated, but I was too scared to tell him.

Throughout that year, we became friends. We shared a few classes, enjoyed similar hobbies, and eventually decided we preferred each other's company to anyone else. We stayed in touch for two years after he graduated, but it wasn't until we both worked on Main Street that we became what we are now.

As for my crush, I continued keeping that to myself. After building such a solid friendship, I was too afraid of ruining it. And though I feel a bit jealous when he dates other girls, it's only because I'm used to having all of his time.

It has nothing to do with envy. Or anger...when I see him kiss someone else.

We're much better as friends. I don't know what I would do if I didn't have Jamie. As much as I've made a big deal about him staying in the car as I confront Patrick, I know he'll come running the moment I need him.

I give him a reassuring smile as I close the door, and he returns it as he rests a toned arm over the back of the seat beside him. It's moments like this when I remember how absurdly attractive he is. It's not that I forget (how could I?), but I'm constantly having to tuck that little observation away.

As I walk slowly up the concrete steps and down the breezeway to Patrick's door, I feel a knot of nervousness forming in my stomach. I made it seem like this wasn't a big deal, but truthfully, I'm worried he won't take it well. Based on previous reactions to less serious situations, I'm prepared for a bout of yelling. He might even punch a wall. But I don't think Patrick would ever physically hurt me.

Would he?

I swallow my nerves and knock twice. Several seconds go by, but I don't hear movement from inside.

Maybe he's not home. *Awesome!* Now I can put it off another day.

Just as I'm about to give up and turn around, I hear a deep, angry voice rising from the parking lot. I walk to the end of the breezeway to glance over the railing, and to my surprise, I see Patrick standing next to Jamie's truck, arms flailing as he animatedly accuses Jamie of trespassing.

"Just great," I mutter to myself. The two of them have not had the best interactions, and it's usually my job to diffuse the situation.

I race carefully back down the stairs and intercept Patrick

before he lands a fist on the hood of Jamie's truck. At the sight of me so close to a swing, Jamie leaps out of the driver's seat and slams the door.

"Back the fuck up," he tells Patrick, his voice low and controlled. I can hear the fury in his tone, something I've never witnessed from him before, but his demeanor is somehow calm, alarmingly calm. He holds his posture steady, eyes fixed on the threat ahead of him—the threat against me. The only hint Jamie's close to losing it is the way he's clenching his fists at his sides.

"Here we go," Patrick chides, throwing his arms wide. "Haven't I told you before, bud? This doesn't concern you." He steps right into Jamie's face and I cringe as he taps a pointer finger on Jamie's toned chest. "I'm the boyfriend. You're the friend. Get it straight."

Patrick has muscles, but he's bulky and unevenly proportioned. Jamie's physique is toned and lean. At first glance, it doesn't look as if he's that strong, but he was lying earlier when he mentioned his lack of upper body strength. I know for a fact he bench presses over three hundred pounds at the gym.

I see the veins in Jamie's neck strain at how hard he's clenching his jaw. But then he smirks, and my stomach drops.

"Correction," he says, and I swear I hear him snarl, "I'm the *best* friend. And you're the ex. *Bud.*"

Patrick's eyes go wide for half a second as he realizes why I'm here, unused to being taken by surprise. Did he truly not expect me to break up with him? Is he that oblivious to his own behavior? Then those baffled eyes shift to me, and I take a step back. Jamie takes my hand and moves me to his side, out of reach in case Patrick chooses to take another swing and aim it at me.

I watch as Patrick's face goes from surprise to anger to smug acceptance. He looks straight into Jamie's scowl but directs his statement at me. "I knew you'd end up fucking him eventually."

Before I can register what's happening, Jamie has Patrick by the throat, and is spinning him around to slam against the side of the truck. Patrick winces, eyes already watering from the pressure Jamie has on his jugular.

"First of all, do *not* speak to her that way," Jamie tells him, no hint of a waver in his tone. "Second, she's done with you. That means from now on, who she fucks is none of your business." He loosens his grip but doesn't release his hold. "And if I hear from anyone you've tried to contact her in any way," he pauses for effect, "you and I are gonna have some one on one time."

Finally, Jamie steps away, and I'm left staring in shock at what I've just witnessed. I have never seen him reach his boiling point before. He has the tendency to be a bit confrontational, but he's never completely lost his temper. Something about what Patrick said must have really set him off.

He was probably just being protective. Jamie has always seen me as a little sister—someone to keep his eye on and stick up for—but something about this was different. More primal. And I'm not sure how to feel about it.

Jamie glances at me but doesn't make eye contact. "Raegan, get in the truck."

I snap out of my shock and make my way around the hood to scurry into the passenger seat. When I've closed the door, Jamie slowly gets inside and buckles his seatbelt, all the while keeping his eye on Patrick.

Feeling salty, I give the asshole a sarcastic shrug of my shoulders as if to say 'what can I do?' as we back out of the parking lot.

As we turn back on to the main road, I look over to Jamie to make sure he's okay. I can tell his anger hasn't had enough time to simmer yet, because his hand is gripping the wheel a little too tight, so I place mine over top. "Thank you."

At the sound of my voice, he relaxes. But his tone is still sharp when he says, "You're coming home with me."

Chapter Four

JAMIE

By the time we make it back to my condo, most of my anger has dissipated and my muscles are no longer contracting. The entire time I was in Patrick's presence, I had to fight the urge to punch him square in his yappy jaw. The guy is a douchebag, and I knew that going into the situation, so why did I let his stupid comment get to me?

Hearing Raegan's name coming out of his mouth was just one straw too far. Hearing him speak about her in such a crude way made my predator instincts want to pounce. I would not, and will never, tolerate anyone disrespecting her. Because she's my friend. Having such a visceral reaction is completely normal. Totally understandable.

Raegan is sitting quietly in her seat when I turn off the engine. I know I've probably made her uncomfortable with the way I acted, but I don't want her to feel that way around me. I'm supposed to be her safe place. She told me so the first time she ever cried in front of me. Knowing this made me feel worthy, like I had a purpose: to always protect her at any cost.

I just never thought I'd be willing to rip someone's throat out for her.

I guess I can classify my lack of control as another symptom. One more thing to blame on my inner monster.

Every lunar cycle I dread the days leading up to the next full moon, when my self-control is forfeited. As the Waxing Gibbous slowly takes its shape, my patience gets thinner, my lustful thoughts become overpowering, and the Jamie that Raegan knows disappears beneath the surface. It's why I try to stay away from her as much as possible during that unpredictable time. I typically stay at the werewolf camp in the woods where I'm able to shift fully when the moon is full in the night sky. I hate every second I'm not myself, but for those few hours under the moonlight, I have to surrender and let nature take the wheel. In that other body, I am no longer Jamie.

I'm just the wolf.

I don't think Raegan realizes I disappear once a month, but sooner or later she's going to put it together. Especially if she's not gone by next Wednesday. I want her to be here—safe and away from Patrick—but I only have four more days until I'll have no choice but to shift.

I take a deep breath and clear my thoughts before turning to look at her. She's pulled her left leg up to rest beneath her on the seat while her right leg is perched on the dash. I've told her before how dangerous the position is, thinking of what could happen if the airbags go off, and when she sees me looking at her, she immediately moves both feet to the floorboard, giving me a sheepish expression like she's in trouble.

Her actions bring a much needed smile to my face, and I think I can finally feel the last ounce of anger fizzle out of my blood stream.

I wish more than anything that I could tell her about what I am. I know I could, if I really wanted to, but the lie has gone so far at this point I wouldn't know how to bring it up. Plus, everything would change, and that's the last thing I want. Especially now when she needs me the most.

She's waiting for me to be the first to speak, so I say the first thing that comes to mind. "I think you should stay here tonight."

She closes her eyes thoughtfully. "I had a feeling you would say that."

"Did Mavis predict it for you?" I joke.

A breeze blows in through her cracked window and I catch the scent of her coconut shampoo. I shudder and have to face my window for a moment so I can catch my breath. She doesn't seem to notice.

"Nope." She pops the P dramatically. "I saw it myself. I have a sixth sense when it comes to these things."

"These things, meaning me," I point out, looking back at her.

She leans in conspiratorially. "Well, yes. What else would it be?"

I shake my head and embrace the better mood she's put me in. "You're pretty good at sensing Kit-Kats as well."

A goofy grin takes over her doll-like features. "You have some don't you?"

I'm momentarily lost in the details of her face. Typically her dark hair is down in loose waves around her face, but today she styled it into a bun at the top of her head. With her hair pulled back, I can easily study the splattering of freckles across her skin and the everpresent rosy undertone of her skin, her button nose and full lips, and her eyes, the most brilliant shade of blue.

I clear my throat and lean over to open the glove compartment in front of her, my arm brushing her knee. Inside is a pack of unopened Kit-Kat bars and Sour Patch Kids—her favorite candy and mine. "I bought these for the movie, but I guess you can have them now," I playfully tease.

She grabs the bag of Kit-Kats and clutches them to her chest like a treasure. I love that the simplest gestures bring her joy.

"Come on," I say, "we'll stay in tonight. We can finish watching that documentary about cheerleaders."

"Ooo yes. That brunette had just broken her ankle and she's definitely not gonna make mat."

She rushes from the truck and darts for the front steps, practically skipping her way to the top to unlock the door, using the key I gave her a few years ago, for if she ever needed to come by when I'm not home. She throws a look over her shoulder to me, a warm smile lighting up her face.

For a moment, I imagine what it would be like if she lived here. I can see her coming home after closing the bookstore to a home cooked dinner I prepared just for her. We'd spend the evening watching our favorite shows, and then we'd go up the stairs hand in hand to get ready for bed.

Where in the fuck is this domestic shit coming from?

Either I'm losing my cool on Raegan's shitty ex or I'm daydreaming about being a stepford wife, nothing in between. The full moon needs to hurry up and get here or else I'm going to go insane.

WE'RE SETTLED on the couch as the credits scroll on the final episode of our current binge watch, and Raegan is fast asleep with her feet tucked into my side. Her head is resting on one of my throw pillows and her mouth is slightly open as she breathes softly in and out into the crook of her arm. I place a hand on her thigh but keep still. It's the most I can touch her before my dick starts whispering in my ear about other plans.

I don't have these thoughts often, and I know I can mostly blame my wolf nature, but sometimes I think there's more to it. I've never had anyone else in my life I could consider a confidant. Someone I can tell all my secrets to and not fear they'll run away screaming. Raegan is the one person I've confided in the most, but still, there's this one little detail about myself I can't seem to confess.

I want to—so badly that some days the pressure eats me alive.

As a werewolf, we're told one of our greatest rewards in life is finding our perfect mate. The one person who fits with you like a puzzle piece and supports you as a beam supports the structure of a home. It doesn't have to be another wolf. Most of the time it isn't. Things are much different now than when my grandparents were going through the traditions of finding a mate. I've known werewolves to mate with vampires and humans. It's not unheard of in this day and age. There's someone out there for all of us, and one day the moment will come when I find mine. But as I gaze upon Raegan's soft features cast in the light of the television screen, I wonder if it could be her.

But wouldn't I know already if we were mates? There have to be signs—some sort of magical firework moment that occurs the moment we touch. But there's nothing. Just my hand on her thigh. Just two best friends watching a movie.

I decide it's time to move Raegan upstairs, because I know she won't want to stay on the couch all night. Another thing we share in common is lower back pain, but I fear that's just a sign of being in our thirties.

I carefully shift to the edge of the couch hoping not to disturb her position so I can stand and stretch, but it's no use. Being the lightest sleeper in the world, she lets out a small moan and rubs her eyes.

"Is it over?" she asks with a yawn.

"You slept through the entire last episode."

She groans and rolls onto her back. "How did it end?"

"They won."

"Did they run into the ocean?"

I laugh because it's the part she's been waiting for from the beginning of the show. "Yes. They ran into the ocean."

"Okay good."

She closes her eyes and I can tell she's about to drift off again, so I nudge her shoulder. "Come on," I coax her. "Let's go upstairs."

The statement sends a shiver down my spine, but I have to remind myself I'm only referring to us going to our own bedrooms. I have a guest room that's just for Raegan, and she's stayed in it so often her smell has clung to every surface. There are extra clothes already in a drawer, and travel size toiletries in the bathroom down the hall.

She groans louder this time, but instead of waiting for her to get up on her own, I slide my arms beneath her limp body and lift her into a cradling position. "I know, I'm ruining every-thing and I'm the worst," I murmur teasingly.

"Admitting is the first step to recovery," she mutters, throwing her arms around my neck and nuzzling into my chest. It's like she's trying to kill me.

I can't help but smile as I carry her up the steps to the second floor.

Her bedroom is cold, just the way she likes. The tempera-ture hasn't dropped enough for me to start using the central heating, so the inside of the house matches the crisp cool air outside. October is the month when autumn truly takes form in Tennessee. Being in the south, the humidity lingers through September, and we can only hope the average temperature will change by Halloween. This year it seems the weather has turned in our favor.

I place her on the bed and pull a blanket from the bottom drawer of the dresser. She'll crawl beneath the comforter eventually, but just in case I drape a quilt over her as she curls up on her side.

As I'm leaving, she calls out softly. "Goodnight."

"Goodnight, Rae," I tell her, closing the door with a soft click. Then I'm off to my bedroom to clear my head before attempting to sleep.

Chapter Five

RAEGAN

I wake up in a bed that's not mine, but it only takes me a moment to realize where I am. I can tell the moment I open my eyes and see the smooth white ceiling above me. The ceilings in my apartment are an ugly beige stucco.

The stiff mattress beneath me only confirms where I am. I shift and hear the creaks and groans of Jamie's guest bed, but really my bed, given I'm the only one who ever stays here. It's nice having a bed after a late movie night when I don't feel like driving home, but would it kill Jamie to update it? I'm pretty sure it's over a hundred years old and is only a few more sleeps away from falling apart.

It's Saturday morning, so my plans for the day are wide open. Part of me wants to stay in all day and avoid the outside world. It's something I tend to do quite a bit, though I know it's not the best coping mechanism.

I've struggled with anxiety my entire adult life, and whenever there's a complicated situation, my way of processing involves avoiding it altogether.

Important phone call? Ignore it and try to forget.

Confrontation with an ex? Hide at my best friend's house for the foreseeable future.

I don't do well when it comes to pressure, and after last night's scuffle between Jamie and Patrick, I think I'll stay in my own little bubble while the world continues on outside my door. At least I'm not alone. Jamie will be here to keep me company. And his streaming subscription.

I toss the covers from my sweaty body and gather what little supplies I have to go take a shower. I have an extra change of clothes that I keep here at all times, but if I'm going to be staying longer than a day, I'll need to go home and pack a bag.

As I pad down the carpeted hall to the bathroom, I hear the whine of the coffee maker, meaning Jamie must be downstairs. I glance at my watch and see I've slept till eleven. Jamie's probably been awake since dawn.

I quietly close the door and proceed to re-tie my hair into a neater bun from where it's come loose throughout the night. Once it's secure, I remove the clothes I slept in last night and step into the shower.

The water is hot against my flushed skin, and I pretend each droplet is washing away the events of yesterday. I never expected Jamie to threaten Patrick the way he did. The sight of his hand clenched around Patrick's throat—loose enough not to truly injure, but tight enough to send a message—infiltrated my dreams as I slept. In my dream, Patrick was a human-sized avocado, and Jamie was the size of a skyscraper, his hand large enough to wrap around Patrick's round body and squeeze all his insides out!

Remembering the dream now is hilarious, but as I tossed and turned throughout the night, it felt more like a nightmare. Jamie being protective has never looked so predatory before. He looked out for me in high school when guys in his grade made fun of my nerdy appearance, and he's never been afraid to be the first to speak up on someone else's behalf. But last night he looked like he was one insult away from crushing Patrick's windpipe.

It wasn't the first time I've heard a comment like that on the close relationship Jamie and I have, though maybe a little less rude. If I had a dollar for every resident of this town who has asked if we're a couple, I'd have enough to take at least a week's vacation from the bookstore.

I understand why some might think we're in a relationship, because, in a way, we are. For me, it's more than a friendship. We're as close and compatible as any couple, we just don't kiss.

Or have sex.

Because that would be weird.

No matter how intriguing it sounds.

With a little too much force, I twist the knob to the off position and step out of the shower. Once I've dried off with a fluffy towel and redressed, I head down the stairs to see what Jamie is up to.

I find him in the kitchen sitting on a stool at the island. His back is facing me, but I can see his favorite coffee cup filled with steaming black coffee. As if he senses me, he turns and greets me with a smile as warm as a hug.

"Hey." His voice is low and scratchy. It's probably the first time he's spoken this morning.

"Hi."

I feel nervous for some reason, as if there's been a shift between us only I can sense. I'm probably still shaken from last night. It's definitely not because of how cute his hair looks rumpled from being pressed against his pillow, or the way his back muscles stretch as he turns back to sip at his coffee.

And why am I suddenly overcome with the need to reach out and touch him? The house feels chilly, and right now I'm craving the warmth of his skin against mine like the lick of a flame on a cold autumn night. A shiver rushes down my spine and my arms pebble with goosebumps.

Get a hold of yourself, Raegan. This is your best friend you're ogling.

When I look back, I'm momentarily entranced by the movement of his throat as he swallows, but as his cup hits the counter I snap back to focus.

Damn it! Stop staring at his Adam's apple.

"How did you sleep?" he asks as I slip clumsily onto the stool across from him.

"Good," I lie. Jamie doesn't need to know about my demented avocado dream.

His lips press together like he wants to ask a followup question, but he diverts to a different topic. "I thought you might want to go grab a few extra clothes later. What time does he get off from the auto repair shop?"

'He' meaning Patrick. It seems Jamie has no interest in saying his name, which is fine with me. "One o'clock, I think." The douche-canoe works part time at Reaper Repairs from eight A.M. to one in the afternoon, then he busts tables at Bones in the evenings. He's typically home for a few hours before going to the restaurant, so we should have a window before and after when I can go to my building uninterrupted and grab my stuff. "Let's go after breakfast," I suggest.

Jamie nods and gets up to make a cup of coffee for me. "I think it's best that you stay here this weekend. Just to let him cool off a bit. I don't like how unpredictable that guy is."

"Okay," I agree. I think about my cat, but I know Cleetus will be fine on his own. I constructed a kitty door within the window that opens onto the balcony. From there he can make it to Mavis's backdoor on the first floor where she feeds the neighborhood strays. As much as she might be annoyed with me, she'd never let a cat go hungry, and I'm grateful she looks out for Cleetus when I'm not home.

"But if you need to stay longer, you know you can." Jamie pours a decent amount of creamer into my mug and sets it in front of me. It's a medium shade of beige, just the way I like.

"I don't think that'll be necessary. Your warning was loud and clear."

He stiffens as he sits back down, then looks me pointedly in the eye, the golden brown color melting away any nerves I felt before, just like honey.

"Listen," he starts, "I'm sorry for how I–"

I cut him off by placing a hand around his as he clutches his mug. "You have nothing to apologize for. I'm grateful you were there. You were right to go with me. Thank you."

He lets out a huge breath, lips parting in relief. "I didn't want to scare you with how I acted."

"You didn't. I promise."

I see his shoulders relax and it brings me relief as well. I can tell how much this weighed on him, but Jamie could never scare me. I trust him irrevocably.

I sit up straight and change the heavy subject. "So, what do you want to do today?"

"Let's just hang out," he says, looking up from his coffee to meet my gaze again. "We haven't done that in a while."

A smile is the only response I need to give him.

Abruptly, my cell phone *chimes* from the living room. I get up to grab my bag, shocked that Patrick is still trying to call me, but when I finally see the screen it's my mother.

I grimace and answer begrudgingly, "Hello, mom."

"Raegan? Oh, good. I caught you."

Her haughty voice comes in a little too loud and clear, so I have to turn the volume down. "What's up?"

"Well," *here we go,* "Mavis called earlier saying you're thinking about ending your lease."

"That's not what I—" I groan. "I told her I'd let her know."

There's a moment of silence. "And?"

I'm trying my best to understand how this concerns my mother, but I'm coming up short. "And then I put the car in drive," I say sarcastically.

I hear a dramatic *humph* through the speaker, and I can imagine she's rolling those scrutinizing eyes of hers to the back of her head. "What did you decide, Raegan?"

Jamie is throwing his hands in the air, silently pleading to know what we're talking about, but I hold up a finger. "That was only a few hours ago," I tell her. "I've got some other stuff I'm dealing with right now." He comes over to where I'm pacing back and forth in the living room and gestures for me to put the phone on speaker, so I do.

I place it on the back of the couch and he leans over the device like an eager child.

"You know your room is still empty," she suggests, her voice laced with sickly sweetness, but I can discern the manipulative tone.

"I don't want to live with the coven."

"There was no reason for you to leave in the first place. I know you're struggling to keep up with rent. Why do you insist on making things harder for yourself when you could live here for free?"

"I like having my own place," I state bluntly.

Ever since I left home at twenty-seven, my mother has been trying to guilt-trip me back under her roof. For some reason, in her mind, I think my not living with the rest of the coven only shines a spotlight on the fact that I'm not a witch. Secretly, I know she's disappointed her only daughter doesn't have magic, but she'll never admit it.

While I think it's her just being selfish, Jamie has tried to convince me that in reality, she just feels left out. All of the other witches her age have daughters to teach their magic to. Sometimes I can see where he's coming from, but then I remember what it was like to live with her.

There was zero space or privacy in that house. As much as I like cozy small spaces, I prefer them alone. And quiet. The coven was constantly full of yelling and things breaking. I had to get out of there the second I could. Plus, I felt out of place. I couldn't relate to anyone else, and the things I was going through as a teenager in high school just didn't matter to the other girls. They could solve all their problems with a spell here and there.

Jamie can see the tension on my face at having to rehash my reasons for leaving all over again, so instead, he takes a step back and pretends he's yelling from the other room.

"Hey, Rae! I think the oven is on fire!"

"Sorry, mom. Jamie's trying to cook again."

I hang up with a relieved sigh, and Jamie wraps his arm around my shoulders, pulling me into his side. "Time for movie night."

So, after stopping by my apartment to grab a few more things, we spend the rest of the day watching movies, trying new recipes from Jamie's food delivery service, and just enjoying one another's company. Throughout the night, I forget about my confusing feelings, and by the time he passes out in the living room after an all day marathon of watching our favorite boy wizard, I'm reminded that at the end of the day, we're just Raegan and Jamie: best friends first.

Everything else comes second.

Chapter Six

JAMIE

The weekend passes quickly—a little too quickly for my liking. Raegan and I were able to stop by her place and gather a few necessities, and it's good we did. On the way to her complex, I caught the subtle iron scent that signals the beginning of her monthly cycle, so I casually suggested she grab supplies in case of an emergency. The next day, when she inevitably started her period, she called me a witch. Rather that than the truth I guess.

Saturday and Sunday was spent mostly hanging around the house. We made two separate runs to the closest market for snacks, but other than that, Raegan opted for staying in. I assumed it was because of how she was feeling, but secretly I think she wanted to stay away from anyone who might ask questions. I had no qualms with this, because it lessened our chances of running into Patrick. My hope is by the time Raegan returns to the bookstore, he will have moved on to his next target.

But now Monday morning is here, and I'm hesitant to let her leave. I know the feeling is ridiculous, and it's just as possessive as Patrick, so I have to remind myself she's a grown woman. Raegan is perfectly capable of taking care of herself, but that doesn't stop me from reminding her I'm only a phone call away.

"Even if your gut tells you something is wrong, you listen to it," I tell her for what feels like the hundredth time.

"I will, Jamie. I swear. But honestly, I think you're overreacting." She closes the lid on the tupperware I lent her for her lunch and slides it into her bag. "Patrick might be overbearing, but he's also lazy. He constantly wanted to know where I was and what I was doing, but he never actually put in the work to see me. He wanted me to come to him. And after what happened Friday, I'm probably too much trouble. I bet he's already moved on to some other insecure girl who will do whatever he says."

I don't like that she backhandedly just referred to herself as being insecure, but I don't push her on it. She slings the straps of her tote over her shoulder, and I follow her to the door. Though she's probably right about Patrick having moved on by now, I refuse to completely let my guard down.

"Besides," she adds, hand reaching for the handle on the front door, "I'm not going to spend the whole day looking over my shoulder. I'm not afraid of him. And I *know* you're not."

I narrow my eyes and give her an unamused expression. "I'm not saying you have to be afraid. Just...be aware."

She nods once, then leans in to kiss my cheek. "I will."

Then she's out the door, and I'm left to deal with my anxious thoughts alone.

I'VE JUST FLIPPED the CLOSED sign to OPEN when I see my friend Aidan strolling down the sidewalk. I head behind the counter to start preparing his usual order: a matcha latte with oat milk and chai syrup. I've teased him endlessly over it, making sure he's aware he orders like a basic bitch, but if there's one thing about Aidan I know for sure, he doesn't give a fuck what anyone thinks.

I hear the bell *ding* just as I'm closing the lid on his to-go cup and look up to see his slow self-assured grin. "I see you were ready and waiting for me as always," Aidan jokes. "Good dog."

Only from Aidan would I accept a jab like that. Maybe Raegan, but she doesn't know what I am. Aidan strolls up to the counter and grabs the cup with his long, pale fingers then lifts it slowly to his lips to take a long drink. As a cold blooded vampire, I know he doesn't feel the same sensations that us warm-blooded mammals do, but damn, he gulps the steaming hot latte as if it were a glass of sweet iced tea.

He lets out a low hum and lifts the cup in a salute. "Warms the soul, doesn't it?"

"As if you have one," I jab back.

He smirks and walks to the bar top to the right of the counter and sits. Aidan Ward has been coming to Double Double every morning for three years. The coffee shop receives plenty of patrons throughout the day, but Aidan is always the first. He claimed once that he prefers the peace and quiet first thing in the morning, but the more I get to know him, I get the feeling he just enjoys my company.

Vampires are some of the more secluded paranormals in Shadow Hills. Even more than the werewolves. Unlike werewolves and witches who choose to live amongst a group, vampires live alone. Witches tend to live with their covens, stuffing themselves into houses like clown cars. Raegan's mother lives with six other witches in a green house at the end of Main Street. Every time I pass the property, I hear a mixture of yelling and laughter, along with the crashing of whatever knickknacks they've accidentally broken that day.

Werewolves are a bit less open, even in a town that welcomes paranormals. When Shadow Hills was first built, it was meant to serve as a place to house the "monsters" from the bigger cities. Creatures like werewolves and vampires became known to the public a little over one hundred years ago, and in the beginning it had been pure chaos. It took years of violence to finally come to a truce with humans agreeing to let all paranormals live in peace, but separate. Thus, Shadow Hills was established. I think despite there being a truce between paranormals and humans, the werewolves still didn't trust in the promises that had been made to protect them. So they created their own territory: a camp within the forest of Shadow Hills.

I had a choice to live with the pack when I first moved to Shadow Hills, but I'd stayed with my parents. After that, the decision just stuck, and I preferred the normalcy of coming home to a house after shifting than being surrounded by wild heathens always causing a ruckus. But there have been times in the lunar cycle when I've preferred to spend my full shift with the pack, needing to expend my pent up energy on another wolf instead of running through the trees alone.

Vampires are completely solitary creatures. I've never seen more than one at a time. Actually, I believe Aidan is the only vampire I know in Shadow Hills. There are more, including a century old teenager I've never had the pleasure of meeting, but they aren't as friendly as Aidan. They are a rare and ancient species, and the act of creating a new vampire is a very tedious process. This makes them all the more interesting to others. It's because of this that I can understand why Aidan prefers to visit before the morning rush, and why I always welcome him.

"Want anything to eat this morning?" I ask as I unlock the displays beneath the register and begin filling them with fresh bagels and various pastries from Bone Appetit Bakery.

Aidan thinks for a moment, his face resembling a smolder more than a thoughtful expression. "Do you still have those delicious mini quiches?"

People are always surprised that vampires eat and drink just like them. Though they need blood to survive, it's far less often than it's made to appear in the movies, and they most definitely hold on to the same cravings they had in their human life, especially Aidan.

"That was a one time special, I'm afraid," I tell him. "You'll have to ask Claudia about those." Claudia is the owner of the bakery, and she provides all our breakfast options.

"Ah yes," Aidan muses, nodding slowly. "The blonde with all the questions."

I smirk. "She's no more curious than anyone else about having a conversation with a vampire. She just has no filter."

"She was very persistent." Aidan pulls his face into a pinched expression and looks to the ceiling as if reliving the experience, then says, "I'll take a scone."

"Coming right up."

I give him the best from the case, golden brown and buttery, then I continue busying myself around the shop. It's quiet for several minutes while Aidan eats his fresh scone, but I hear him hum in curiosity.

Thinking there's something wrong with the food, I turn to face him, but he's merely taking in the area around him. "You haven't decorated the shop yet."

"Raegan pitched a mad scientist theme to me this year, but she knows better."

"As long as I've been coming here," Aidan drawls, "and nary a simple jack-o-lantern."

"You're damn right," I jest, scowling at my empty windows, imagining a cluster of pumpkins and a scarecrow crowding the space. Aidan smirks.

All of the businesses in town are gearing up for the Founding Day Festival. Booths line the main road for each local business to feature their signature wares amongst music and games. The locals are even more dedicated to the tradition than the tourists, especially the paranormals.

Everyone leans into the outside stereotypes that are thrust upon us. The ghosts wear chains and bedsheets with cut outs for eyes and a mouth, the witches wear pointy hats and carry around broomsticks, and a few of the pack members attend donning wolf masks from a party supply store. It's a way for us to poke fun at ourselves while also calling attention to the absurd stories humans tell.

I've never truly attended the festival before, having been responsible for manning the Double Double booth and serving everyone hot chocolate, chai lattes, and spiced cider. I refuse to serve such fru-fru drinks at the shop, but the festival is the one time I allow it. It always goes over well, and I'm *always* told I need to add them to the menu, but I refuse. My coffee shop is not cutesy. It's refined, maintaining a certain sophisticated aesthetic. The walls are painted a deep burgundy and accented with dark mahogany trim, strings of warm lights are strategically hung across the ceiling, illuminating the front counter and various other displays around the shop, and the walls are accented with gold and bronze antique knick knacks and a handful of vintage mirrors I found at garage sales. Raegan says it gives *medium* academia vibes, whatever that means.

It's a quarter after eight in the morning when the next customer comes in, and by this point Aidan has already stood from his seat and placed several bills in the tip jar. He gives me a curt nod as he heads for the door, but just as the bell *dings* above him, I hear something else filter in past the early morning sounds of birds chirping and shop owners opening their doors.

A voice—Raegan's voice—and it's in distress.

Aidan must have heard it, too. He halts on the threshold, head slightly turned to look at me and gauge my reaction. He has no idea about what happened with Patrick, but I must have managed to communicate the seriousness of the situation by the panic in my eyes, because Aidan darts across the room in the blink of an eye and is now right in front of me. "That sounded like Raegan."

As much as I hate to admit it, I know he's faster than me. Aidan's glaring eyes are telling me as much as he waits for me to react, or at least say something. But I'm glued to the spot. I hadn't realized that in a fight or flight situation I would end up freezing.

I manage to speak one word as I strip off my apron and toss it onto the counter. "Go."

Aidan splits from the premises in a blur of motion, the door left ajar from where he ran through it at top speed.

My single patron is rooted to the spot, rapidly blinking and mouth gaping with words she can't get out. I don't take the time to explain what just happened. Instead, I race down the street after Aiden, wishing for the first time for a power I don't have. I'm fast, but not vampire fast. I just hope whatever's happening, Aidan is already there to stop it.

I never should have let Raegan out of my sight.

Chapter Seven

RAEGAN

I have never been this angry at someone before. And frustrated. No matter what I say to this man, I can't make him see reason.

"Raegan, come on," he drones, drawing out the words. "You know we're good together. You felt it on our first date. It's that bitch of a best friend of yours whispering lies about me in your ear, isn't it?"

Patrick refuses to accept the words I've repeated not once, not twice, but three times. And now I'm yelling it for a fourth. Because apparently, I'm in just as much denial as he is.

What is it called when you do something over and over and expect a different result? Oh yeah, insanity.

This idiot is driving me insane.

He's obviously drunk. He's barely keeping his balance without a hand against the brick wall of Bound and Buried. I was minding my own business, simultaneously counting inventory while making a mental note of the books I need to buy, when Ethan stomped over irritably to tell me there's a man pacing back and forth in front of the store and giving 'bad juju'.

My first reaction after seeing Patrick through the front window swaying from foot to foot with sweat dripping from his temples was to smack my palm flat against my forehead. Clearly he didn't get Jamie's message like I thought he did. I didn't even ask myself what the hell he was thinking, because I already knew. The dipshit knew the only way to get my full attention would be to catch me at work, without Jamie.

Now I'm standing on the sidewalk, embarrassing myself in front of all the other small business owners, as I try to talk some sense into this basket case of a man. I need to coax him into the side alley between the book store and Claudia's bakery, so we aren't in front of so many prying eyes.

"Patrick," I start again, taking a tentative step toward him like he's a wild animal that's gotten loose in the streets, "let's talk somewhere private. Just you and me."

I'm hoping he'll take this as a sign he's won me over. After all, getting me alone is what he was aiming at to begin with. Miraculously, he actually starts to follow me into the alley, though I don't think he realizes he's doing it. He's so drunk I could probably steal his shoes right now and he'd have no idea.

I lace my voice with a fake dulcet tone. "I know technically I didn't get a chance to break up with you, because, well, Jamie did it for me, but it's the truth." Now that the words are out, there's no point backtracking, so I plow forward. "I just don't see this working out. And after the way you've acted today, you're only confirming my choice. Because that's what it is: my choice. I need you to respect that."

Patrick stares at me with busted pupils and nostrils flaring. I can see it's taking him a second to process what I'm saying, but once he does, his veins cord under his skin. He looks enraged.

But then he reaches out as if to brush a hand across my cheek, and I quickly step away, shouting, "Don't touch me!"

But he's moving much faster than I thought he would be capable of in his inebriated state, and now he's got his hands around my throat. "You belong to me!" he bellows.

I screech as he squeezes the air from my lungs. I attempt to claw at his fingers as they dig into my flesh, but it's becoming harder and harder to take a breath. Black spots dance around the edges of my vision, but just when I think I've made a terrible mistake being alone with Patrick, my lungs expand and I'm breathing fresh air.

I gasp and run a hand over my already aching throat, but I have no idea how I'm standing here. Where is Patrick?

Then I see him. Jamie's friend, Aidan, is standing above Patrick with a menacing scowl. At the speed he just moved he should be breathing heavily or sweating profusely, but he's perfectly poised. He leans over Patrick's confused face and slowly cocks his head.

"What do we have here?" Aidan says, wrinkling his nose in disgust.

Patrick scrambles to his feet and plants them widely with his shoulders back. He looks like he's about to try and fight a vampire, but surely he can't be serious.

Aidan smirks in clear amusement. "*Please*," he pleads in a mocking tone. He holds both hands up in fake surrender. "I beg you."

Patrick takes a swing, but it never lands. Instead, his fist comes to a screeching halt as it's caught in Jamie's strong hand.

Where the fuck did he come from?

Aidan is preternaturally fast, but how the hell did Jamie get here so quickly? He's standing just over Aidan's right shoulder, and together they look like the stars of a superhero crossover special.

Aidan hasn't even flinched, but Patrick's eyes are now bulging from their sockets. A harried, wild expression takes over his features, and I see the fist trapped in Jamie's grip start to shake.

If I weren't so shaken by almost being strangled, I'd be incredibly impressed. Aidan must have heard me shout and come straight here. But how did Jamie know something was wrong? There's no way he could have heard me from down the street and inside his shop.

Jamie shifts his gaze over to me, assumingly to make sure I'm alright, but when his eyes drop to my throat, his pupils burst with fury. There must already be a visible mark there, because suddenly, Jamie is yanking Patrick by the back of his sweaty collar, and I swear I see the guy's toes barely touch the ground. I knew Jamie was strong, but not superhuman strong. Yet somehow he's holding Patrick's entire body weight, with one arm, without straining a muscle.

"What did I tell you about contacting her ever again?" Jamie rebukes.

I would expect the question to be rhetorical, but Jamie is clearly waiting for an answer. He clutches Patrick's shirt even tighter, slowly choking him just as Patrick had choked me.

He asks again, this time clenching his teeth. "*What* did I tell you?"

Patrick wheezes. "We'd have—*ah*—we'd have a...one on one."

"Why don't we go do that now?"

Jamie finally lets Patrick touch the ground, but then he starts shuffling him out of the alleyway and back onto the street.

"Oh, no," I groan. Like hell are they going to handle this in front of my place of business. "Jamie, wait!"

But it's Aidan's hand on Jamie's shoulder that halts him in place. "Think about what you're doing," Aidan suggests in a low tone. "You know the consequences. People are already curious."

Both he and Jamie glance across the street at the handful of townspeople watching the public disruption in their morning routines. Even worse, when I step back onto the sidewalk, Claudia is standing outside the bakery, watching our every move.

I definitely don't want this confrontation to spill out onto the street, but Aidan looks particularly concerned about Jamie's hand still clutching the back of Patrick's collar.

Is Aidan worried he'll be blamed for this? Back when the laws of Shadow Hills were established, the appointed sheriff at the time knew it would be inevitable for some paranormals to fight others. Over the years, we've let the confrontations settle themselves, as long as they've been fair. But if a paranormal uses a biological advantage over a human, *that* is cause for punishment.

Even if someone does try to say Aidan started the fight, I'm a witness, and I'll tell the truth about the whole incident.

So why does Jamie look afraid?

He lets go of Patrick just as someone points to Kiki's Cafe where Mayor Musthaven is now exiting and crossing the street. One glance at the small crowd that's formed in front of the bookstore, and the mayor is floating over to inspect the scene.

He's a portly ghost, having gained more weight in the afterlife than his human life somehow, though I'm pretty sure it's those sugary pancakes he eats every morning at Kiki's. He floats through the group of people blocking his way before they have a chance to move, each person gasping from the sudden chill from feeling a ghost pass through them uninvited.

"What's going on here?" the mayor asks with a bellowing voice. Everyone stops what they're doing as if they're the ones in trouble, but no one answers his question. Aidan and Jamie are still standing awkwardly on either side of a terrified Patrick who's crumbled to his knees on the sidewalk.

Mayor Musthaven sucks in imaginary air in a dramatic gasp. "Oh my."

The timing is comical, but I have no desire to laugh about any of this. Everyone else is still taking in the scene while I try to find the right words to explain the situation, but Aidan speaks up first.

"August," Aidan addresses the mayor in a personal but stately manner. "You've arrived just in time. We were just assisting Miss Baker with a rather unfortunate incident."

He speaks as if he is above the situation, but not the people. It's a fine line to balance, but being over a century old, I would imagine speaking to people in the proper way becomes second nature.

"What is this human man doing on the ground?" Musthaven asks.

Jamie opens his mouth to say something, but Aidan places a steady hand on his shoulder. It's clear Jamie is still fuming, and there's no doubt whatever comment he planned on making would only make the situation worse.

"Well, you see," Aidan begins, "I came upon Miss Baker here," he gestures to me, still gaping like a floundering fish, "and she appeared to be in distress. It was clear this man was invading her personal boundaries. So, I asked if she needed help, and she informed me that this man has been stalking her for some time. Before I could confront him about this, he attacked her. You can see the bruise already starting to form on her throat."

I'm pretty sure most of the people here know I've been on a few dates with Patrick. They've seen us together at Bones, and Mavis definitely saw me entering his apartment multiple times. I can only imagine what they're thinking now.

Poor Raegan. Taken advantage of.

Poor Raegan. Look what mess she's gotten herself into.

I look at Claudia who's been leaning casually against the brick wall of her bakery since the raucous began. She gives me a pitying smile, only confirming my suspicions.

"Is this true?"

At first I don't realize Mayor Musthaven has directed the question at me, but I quickly recover and nod my head. I can't form words right now. I don't trust them not to fuck up the eloquent explanation Aidan so cleverly concocted. I don't know why, but he's purposefully left Jamie out of the story.

"In that case," the mayor continues, "thank you for intervening." He then turns to Twitty Simmons, the quiet and mouse-like sheriff I hadn't even noticed was there. "Twitty, can you please escort this man to the station?"

The sheriff steps to attention as if he's ready to salute. His dark beard and mustache cover most of his face, but his eyes light up at the command from the mayor.

"I'll come with you," Aidan insists. "I'm sure you need a proper statement."

"Thank you, Mister Ward." The mayor nods his approval before continuing. "By the way, I wanted to chat with you about the walking trail expansion at the park. You mentioned before that you'd be interested in making a sizable donation?"

"Absolutely," Aidan confirms as they head toward the police station side by side like old friends.

Meanwhile, Sheriff Simmons takes Patrick by the arm and pulls him to his feet.

"Y'all can't be serious?" Patrick protests. He starts playing to the crowd, hoping one of them will speak up. "You saw what he did! He used his strength against me! He can't do that!"

"That only applies to paranormals, son," Twitty politely informs him.

I feel my stomach drop to my toes as Patrick passes in front of me. He looks me straight in the eye and says, "You know what he is, don't you? You're gonna regret this, Raegan!"

The rational part of my brain knows he's just acting out. He's trying to say anything he can to get out of the trouble he's caused. But when I look at Jamie, his face isn't all that reassuring. Instead, he looks distressed. Like he's made a terrible mistake. And for the first time ever, I question whether or not he's keeping something from me.

I take a step toward him in need of a simple explanation, but he's already walking back to Double Double. He doesn't even look at me, only strides determinedly down the sidewalk without a second glance, and I feel something inside me break a little.

It feels like we're in a fight, only…I don't know what either of us has done wrong.

I feel a light touch on my elbow and see Claudia beside me. "Are you alright?"

I nod without truly answering, my hand pressed to the tender skin at the base of my throat. If not for the physical mark Patrick has probably left behind, none of this would feel real.

Claudia moves to stand in front of me, forcing herself into my line of sight. "You should go get checked out at the clinic," she says, but I'm not really listening. Instead, my entire focus remains on Jamie as he heads back to Double Double, his form slowly fading into the crowd until I can no longer see him.

I understand he has a business to run, but he couldn't spare a few minutes to come check on me? Compared to his overprotective behavior lately, this feels extremely out of character. This on top of what Patrick just spewed at me, it makes me wonder what's really going on.

I'm confused and angry, but most of all I'm hurt, seeing him walk away.

"Come on," Claudia insists, taking my hand, "I'll go with you."

I lean into her slender frame instinctively, seeking some sort of comfort. Then I let her steer me to her car around the corner and together we drive to the clinic on the other side of town.

Chapter Eight

JAMIE

I try to focus on work for the rest of the day, but everyone who comes into Double Double wants to know about the "brawl" that happened in front of Bound and Buried. No one seems to know exactly what happened, and I've heard everything from Patrick hanging the sheriff upside down by his ankles (I have no idea how that scenario got so mixed up) to Ethan and Aidan getting into a shouting match over Raegan.

I have no intention of setting anyone straight, so I just nod along or shrug and claim I don't know anything. Because somehow, throughout all the chaos, no one seems to be talking about me. It's as if the few who had a front row seat mutually decided to redact me from the plot. Or they just forgot I was there.

I really hope it's the latter, because if they think they're doing me a favor, they're wrong. Pretending I wasn't involved suggests I have something to hide, and once people start catching on, they'll start to ask questions.

I can't believe I let some pathetic asshole, whose worth amounts to less than the dirt on my shoe, get inside my head. Though I can't deny the fact I dropped the ball when it comes

52

to overestimating the size of his balls, I didn't think Patrick would really try anything. I assumed he was all bark and no bite, but apparently I was wrong.

It's not that Patrick is even an actual threat—I could break him like a twig without blinking—but one look at Raegan and the marks he'd left around her neck, and I was seeing pure red.

I've *never* felt so territorial before. I felt this innate need to protect and piss all over her to mark my property, but that would be totally insane. Probably also illegal? *How do you ask for consent to pee on someone?* So instead, I opted for killing him. I was very close to doing just that when the mayor casually stepped in. The sheriff is typically clueless when it comes to the true goings on in this town, but Mayor Musthaven is like a hawk. He's been the mayor of Shadow Hills since its founding, and little happens without his knowledge.

I lost control.

I didn't think about who was watching or what any of them thought. Their opinions meant nothing, as long as I got my revenge on the prick who hurt my girl.

My girl.

That's the thing, isn't it?

She's not really mine, and I'm starting to lose track of all the reasons why.

Because she doesn't see you that way, I remind myself. *And you've never told her you're a frickin' werewolf!*

As much as I wanted to go straight to Raegan's side, I had to get out of there. Knowing Patrick's hands had been on her made the wolf inside me nearly claw its way out from under my skin. Patrick's fingerprints on her skin were like a taunt begging me to mark her myself. I wanted to kill Patrick and claim her as mine right then and there, in front of the entire town. No one would touch her after that.

I would have if Aidan hadn't stopped me. I knew I was

walking a very thin line with so many eyes watching the scene unfold, but my blood was pumping so loudly in my ears it blocked out all the other voices, except for his. If not for Aidan, I would've made a mistake I couldn't turn back from.

It isn't just that I've hidden the truth from Raegan. All paranormals are supposed to be registered in Shadow Hills, but I never did. My parents reached out to my uncle, the alpha of the Shadow Hills pack, and informed him about my first shift, but that information was never passed on to the mayor—or anyone else for that matter—and I never said anything. I think, at the time, I convinced myself that if the paperwork was never filed, that meant my wolf didn't exist, and I could keep on ignoring what I am.

Hiding things from Raegan, however, was more of an accident.

The whole situation is kinda ridiculous if you ask me, but the lie has gone on for so long that it would be too disruptive to bring it up now. You know when someone gets your name wrong when you first meet, but you don't correct them, and then three months later they're still calling you by the wrong name? It's almost impossible to correct them after that, because there's just no good time to bring it up.

That's what it feels like hiding what I am, only a lot more difficult.

The first time I met Raegan was in the high school court-yard where she would take me on a guided tour of campus. We hit it off pretty well. Our banter felt natural, and she was easy to talk to about nothing and everything at the same time. She mentioned her mother was a witch, and in that moment, I was seconds away from telling her I was a paranormal too. But the conversation got away from me, and the words just never came out.

The memory flashes before me as I pour my hundredth cup of coffee of the day.

"SO YOU'RE A—" I start to ask, but she answers my question before I've fully asked it.

The girl is not afraid of speaking her mind, and I find I'm appreciating her confidence compared to other girls her age. She's two grades below me, but I feel as if I share more in common with her than my fellow seniors.

"Oh god no," she says exasperatedly. "Just your everyday boring human." She laughs and waves a hand flippantly as if to say 'Here I am!' "I prefer it, honestly," she adds, "The paranormals in my family are way too much drama. It's nice being normal, don't you think?"

My words are frozen on my tongue, but my head is nodding anyway. I've somehow agreed without realizing and now she thinks I'm human. There's absolutely nothing wrong with being human. I even find myself sharing her opinion of how simple life is without paranormal gifts, because it is. It was.

Before my seventeenth birthday, everything made sense. Now my world has turned upside down, and I'm lying about it in the only place I shouldn't have to.

I COME BACK to reality when I feel the sting of hot liquid spilling over my hand. I yank it back, almost spilling the overfilled cup in the process. "Damn it!"

"You okay?" my barista Casey asks. They're our newest pack member and part of the privied group who knows the truth about me.

"I'm good." I shake out my burning hand. The skin is red, so I shove it beneath a stream of cold water in the sink. The pain subsides momentarily, but I'll have to cover it if I want to keep working, and that's going to sting. I try to remember if I have anything to treat it with when the door *dings* and I see Raegan walk up to the counter.

I look up to meet her beautiful, bright blue eyes and see they're sad.

"What happened?" She steps in front of the line of patrons and leans forward to pull my hand across the counter. As she inspects it, I'm pressed flush against the cash register.

"Raegan, I'm fine. Just a little coffee spillage."

"Do you have mustard?" she asks.

"Why would I have mustard?"

"For sandwiches."

"I don't sell sandwiches."

"You should." She huffs and almost shoves my hand back across the counter.

Okay, I'm guessing she's upset.

"Kiki's is right across the street." I'm so lost in our back and forth that I forget what we're even talking about. "What does mustard have to do with this?" I hold up my stinging left hand.

"The acidity counteracts the burn," she explains.

"That's actually a myth," Casey interjects. "I think it's bad to do that."

Raegan and I look at them with mild shock. The fact this kid said more than three words is probably bigger news than what happened with Patrick, but I shake it off quickly.

I motion for Raegan to follow me to the stockroom, leaving Casey alone with a line of nosey patrons, their face mirroring that of an abandoned puppy.

Raegan and I enter my office to the right of the storage area and close the door. It's a cramped space, no bigger than the size of a walk-in closet, so when we sit down our knees are wedged between one another. I pull a first aid kit from the bottom drawer of my desk and open it. There's a box of bandaids, an expired tube of ointment, and a roll of gauze with about five inches of material left on the roll. I look at the scant supplies, wondering just how much Raegan is judging me right now. I don't ever remember using this kit let alone using everything in it. *Did I even buy this, or was it here before I bought the shop? How old is that ointment?*

"I think mustard is probably safer than this shit," Raegan grumbles, inspecting the crusted tube and prying the top off. Guess she agrees with me. She curls her lip at the sight of the dark brown and unknown substance in the tube then chucks it in the trash.

"I guess we're even now."

Raegan doesn't say anything as she starts digging in her bag. She pulls out a rather large pouch and unzips it to reveal a treasure trove of emergency supplies. I lean closer and see she's got a pair of tweezers, a pack of tissues, mints, nausea medicine, a single period pad, a travel-size bottle of lotion and...aloe?

I fall back against my swivel chair and smile. "You seriously carry aloe around everywhere?" I tease, hoping for some sort of response this time.

"It's for sunburns," she says, tone clipped. "But it also comes in handy for coffee burns." Her smirk is cute as hell, but I'd rather be looking at a full smile. Those are as bright as the sun, and I could stare straight into it all day.

She squeezes a dot of the green goop onto my reddened skin and the cooling sensation instantly soothes the burn. "And yes," she adds, twisting the top back on the bottle. "I guess this makes us even."

I glance at the little pink line on her left forearm that will probably be a scar. "This wasn't your fault though," I tell her, gesturing to the burn she's now wrapping with the last of the gauze. "I did this to myself."

Her brow furrows. "It's not like you did it on purpose. Either time," she offers. "Besides, now you know you need to restock your first aid kit."

She takes in the messy shelves and cluttered papers across my desk. I don't spend much time here, mostly because there's no vent in this room so it gets too damn hot, but the times I do I just drop whatever I'm working on wherever there's space.

For a moment, I think I see tears brimming in her eyes, but she quickly blinks and by the time our eyes meet again she's tucked her lower lip beneath her teeth and changed her expression. "I came to make sure you were okay after what happened, but apparently you're self-harming."

I know it's an attempt at dark humor, but I see the genuine concern lingering in her eyes.

"I'm fine," I promise, though it's a big fat lie.

How I feel right now shouldn't matter. I'm the one who should be checking in on her, but I'm weak.

"You've been a bit on edge lately." She fidgets with her hands, wringing them together like I've seen her do a thousand times when something is on her mind. After a quick internet search, I learned it's a method of self-soothing, something she does when her anxiety is rearing its ugly head. "I know this thing with Patrick has been a lot, and I'm so sorry I've dragged you into it—"

"You didn't drag me into anything." I place my hand over hers and she stops fidgeting. "None of this is your fault. That guy hid his ugliness so he could reel you in. You couldn't have known."

I need her to know there's no reason for her to carry this burden.

She sighs and tells me what I want to hear. "Yeah I know." Unfortunately, I don't think I believe her anymore than she does. "So you're not mad?"

Her question stuns me. "Why would I be mad?"

She hangs her head. "I know you're angry because of what Patrick did, but why did you avoid me?"

I inhale sharply and feel my heart plummet to my core. The hurt look on Raegan's face has me seconds away from spilling my guts right here and now. But what can I do?

I can't tell her why I really walked away, so I say the closest thing I can to the truth.

I take her cheek in my uninjured hand and use the thumb from my other hand to lightly draw a line along the column of her throat where the red marks are already beginning to darken after only a few hours. The dark red hues look like paint I could wipe away with my fingers, but I can't.

"Rae, I'm so sorry," I tell her, jaw tight. I force myself to relax. "You're right. I was mad. I've never been so angry in my life." I gulp. "When I saw what he did, I felt like I was going to lose control. I wanted to kill him, Raegan. I really did. So I had to walk away. But I never meant to walk away from you."

Her lips part, and I want so badly to lean in further to meet them with mine. I sense her heart beating faster, and when I trail my hand down her arm, I feel her tremble.

Then her eyebrows lift and she shoots to her feet. "Welp, I guess we cleared that up. You're good to go." Her tone has suddenly gone from crestfallen to chipper in a matter of seconds. And the desire I thought I saw has dissipated.

We're so close her torso is right in line with my face. I want to grab her hips and pull her into my lap. Luckily my brain catches up to my dick and I stand. I know she felt whatever that moment was between us, but right now she's choosing to ignore it, so I have to respect that.

I lean past her to open the door, and I catch the most glorious scent in the world: coconut shampoo and the underlying sweetness of her natural scent.

I linger and breathe her in for a beat too long, and her voice has to snap me back to reality.

"I remember the first time I opened a door," she teases.

It's disorienting, like the banging of symbols right in my ear, but I recover quickly. The door opens out into the hall, and we're met with the cool circulated air of the AC system.

Before she leaves, I grab her arm and gently trace my thumb against the goosebumps on her skin. "Did you go to the clinic?"

Raegan tilts her head and emphatically answers, "Yeah, of course. I'm fine."

She leans back a bit, creating more space between us, and suddenly I'm cold, a massive contrast to the heat we just shared in my tiny office.

"Are you sure? Rae, he choked you."

Her hand reaches for her throat but stops, instead choosing to wave flippantly and brush my comment away. "It's fine. It wasn't very long. Aidan got there just in time." Then her eyes narrow. "Did you tell him about Patrick?"

"No." I answer truthfully. "He was just in the right place at the right time."

She nods curtly and turns to go. This time I let her.

Before she reaches the swinging door that leads to the front end of the shop, I ask her one last question. "Are you coming back to my house tonight?"

Raegan shakes her head and answers without turning. "I'm gonna go home. Cleetus will be worried."

Chapter Nine

RAEGAN

I've been hiding my panic since Patrick's threat as he was dragged off by Sheriff Simmons. As much as I wanted to confront Jamie directly about the odd warning, I found myself getting distracted by Jamie's distress.

'You know what he is, don't you?'

Something has been off about him lately, like there's a demon he's fighting that resides just below his skin. I want so badly to reach out and help him in any way I can, but Jamie clearly doesn't want to address it. Instead, he's focusing all of his energy on me. Clearly we're very similar in that regard.

After leaving the clinic, I tried to return to work, but Ethan told me to go home because of the influx of customers coming into the store just to ask about the incident. So instead, I gathered my courage and headed for the coffee shop, but talking with Jamie didn't make me feel any better.

Our interaction only made me more confused. Ever since that first incident with Patrick, being around Jamie feels like standing too close to a hot stove. It's a confusing feeling, because the warmth draws me in with a false sense of comfort, but I know if I step too close I'll just get burned. I have to remind myself that this odd attraction I've been feeling is only temporary. Soon this upheaval of normal life will pass, and Jamie and I will go back to the way things were.

But as I'm leaving Double Double, I notice it's becoming harder to breathe. It's like Patrick's hands are still locked around my throat and I can't escape them. I feel a wave of nausea come over me as I reach the corner of 4th and Main, so I close my eyes and take a deep breath, but when I open them again the brightness of the sun sends a sharp pain behind my sockets. It's like a spotlight shining on my panic. I walk quickly around the back of the library as vehicles circle the roundabout to my right.

Once I find my car, I slip inside, twist the key, yank the gear shift into drive, and pull out hastily, running a stop sign.

My breaths come a little easier inside my small sedan than out on the street, but I need to be in my safe place: in my bed and under the covers, door shut and windows closed. It's only eleven A.M. and it already feels like the longest day of my life. I just want to escape the outside world and seek refuge where no one can see me—where no one can ask me if I'm okay, because I'm not.

I speed past the pharmacy and my old high school, and in less than five minutes I've made it to my apartment. I rush up the stairs and head inside, quickly locking the door behind me.

I'm home.

This fact alone should relieve the aching pressure in my chest, but it doesn't. It's not enough. So I grab a bottle of water from the fridge and close myself in my bedroom. I click my bedside lamp on and close the blackout curtains. The subtle, warm light feels better than the harsh sunlight, but I'm not safe yet. I kick off my shoes and pull the covers back so I can climb into bed, but then I hear a scratch at the door and a concerned *meow* from the other side.

"Sorry, Cleetus." I crack the door to let him in, leaving it slightly ajar in case he needs to get out again.

I get in bed fully clothed and pull the blankets to my chest, leaving the weighted blanket over my legs. Cleetus immediately jumps onto the bed and starts pawing at the fluffy material of my duvet. When he's done making biscuits, he curls atop my feet and settles.

I close my eyes and breathe. This time it works.

I am safe. I am secure, I tell myself. *All of my worries are outside, and I'm in here where they can't get me.*

I remember the first time something like this happened. It was my senior year and time was running out to apply to colleges. There aren't many higher education options close to Shadow Hills, and the idea of having to move far from home was too stressful to think about. My mother tried to convince me that it only seemed scary because I'd never been anywhere outside of my hometown before, but once I did, it would be exciting. As much as I wanted to believe her, I couldn't. She never really understood my anxiety and the havoc it sometimes wrought on my mental health. She's never really understood *me.*

I ended up locking myself in my room and putting off filling out applications until it was too late. I didn't end up going to college. Instead, I stayed in Shadow Hills and started working. I don't regret it, but sometimes I do wonder how different my life would have been if I'd decided to leave.

I hear a *ping* from my cell phone and see an unread text. It's most likely Jamie, asking if I made it home alright, so I reach to send a quick reply. But the name on the screen surprises me. It's not my mother, or Patrick, but my friend Joanna.

MONDAY 11:13 A.M. Hey girl, I heard about what happened today. I'm so sorry. Is there anything I can do?

We haven't spoken in a couple months—not since she stopped working at Bound and Buried. That's where we first met. At the time, she was an assistant manager, and I was just a part time clerk. My first day working at the store was our first shift together, and she could see I was uncomfortable dealing with customers. She went out of her way to make me feel more at ease.

As great as she was at leading others and dealing with the occasional customer frustration, eventually she decided to take a leap and quit to run a dog rescue full time, so I was given her position. I admire her heart and commitment to her passion. Not to mention she's one of the nicest people on the planet, yet can still call you on your bullshit.

Her upbeat attitude and constant sarcasm always used to brighten my mood. We grew pretty close while working together, but we haven't hung out since she left the bookstore. The fact that she took the time to check in on me means so much, it actually makes me feel bad about not reaching out sooner.

I shoot her a quick reply, thanking her for her concern and letting her know I'm alright. Before putting my phone away, I send another text, asking if she would want to hang out soon.

Switching the ringer off, I settle back into bed. With the feel of my weighted blanket holding me down, and Cleetus's warm body against mine, I am finally able to relax. I stay like this until I fall asleep.

Because my phone is on silent, I don't hear when Jamie calls at noon, or the ten times after that.

. . .

I WAKE up to a warm hand against my cheek, but it doesn't startle me. I know it's Jamie just from his touch—the calluses on his palm from lifting weights and the path his thumb takes as it draws circles against my skin.

"What time is it?" I ask hoarsely.

I don't open my eyes, but I imagine he's frowning. "It's five thirty. Have you been asleep this whole time?"

The last time I looked at the clock it said eleven fifteen.

I roll over and see he's right. I slept almost seven hours.

As I rub my eyes and stretch, extending my legs now that Cleetus is no longer at the foot of the bed, I remember flashes of another dream I had about Jamie. This time he wasn't a giant but a dog. Or maybe a wolf. It was just the two of us, me sitting on a bench in front of the water at the park and wolf-Jamie curled at my feet like Cleetus. I took him for a walk around the walking trail, but he kept pulling at his leash and almost getting away from me.

I brush it off as just another odd way my brain is trying to sort out my stress, but then Jamie's face comes into view.

He's sitting on the edge of the bed, my bedside lamp illuminating the left side of his face while the other is shadowed. He leans in closer and moves his unbandaged hand to my forehead as if to check for a temperature.

"I'm okay," I tell him. I've been saying that a lot lately, still pretending to make everyone worry less. I shift to a sitting position and lean back against the headboard, keeping the covers pulled over my torso.

I've never had such a severe panic attack in front of Jamie before. He's seen me approach that line, but I've never crossed it with him around. When my anxiety is at an all-time high, I have to go somewhere small. My room has always been my safe place. It was at my parents house, and it is now, here in my tiny apartment. It's why I've never complained about the size. I prefer it this way. The closed-in space is like an embrace.

One of the reasons I've never accepted Jamie's offer to move in with him is because I worry about his condo being too big. It seems silly, but it's a genuine fear. In the midst of an anxiety attack, I would never be able to go downstairs to get water, or even walk down the hall to go to the bathroom. Here, I have everything just a few steps away. The guest room is fine when I'm staying for the weekend, but if I moved in, it would take a while for that space to feel completely safe. To feel like *mine*.

Jamie is watching me carefully as I sort through my current thoughts. He knows I'm spiraling, but I have to explain why I'm in bed or else he's going to think something is seriously wrong.

"Are you sure?" he asks, still needing confirmation that I'm not sick with the flu or something.

I nod. "I just get like this sometimes," I try to explain. "It's not a big deal."

Jamie narrows his eyes and removes his hand. "Uh huh," he says, disbelieving. "Try again."

My head falls back with a thump against the headboard and I sigh. "It's an anxiety thing. This thing with Patrick is stressing me out. I don't like what he's doing to our relationship." The admission slips out accidentally, but I keep going. "It's like he's putting an unnecessary strain on our friendship," I continue, purposely changing the word and hoping Jamie won't notice. "I can't help but worry. You've been...different. I feel like you're keeping something from me."

Though it's true that Jamie's domineering and aggressive nature has been shocking, I have to admit to myself that it's also been intriguing. Something has changed between us, and the only factor I keep coming back to is Patrick, yet I haven't quite put my finger on it.

Jamie's expression changes to something like guilt. He pulls back and clears his throat. "Raegan, listen," he begins, but Cleetus startles us both by jumping up onto the bed between us. He must have heard us talking and come to investigate.

"Hi, baby boy," I mew, scratching his cheeks and under his chin. He purrs happily and rubs his face against mine.

Jamie stands up, and Cleetus turns to face him like a guard dog. Jamie holds his hands up in surrender. "I'm just going to get your mother some fresh water. At ease, soldier." He takes my still full water bottle and leaves my room. He's probably going to dump more ice cubes in it. He knows I like my water to be cold.

Cleetus turns back to face me and I give him a reassuring kiss on the forehead. "I'm okay, honey. I promise." He seems to accept this because he leaps from the bed over to my bookshelf and lounges along the top shelf to casually keep an eye on things.

Jamie comes back a minute later with a clinking water bottle and a pre-packaged peanut butter and jelly sandwich from the fridge. I take the snack and unwrap it.

Instead of sitting on the edge like he did before, he plops down beside me on the other side of the bed. He toes off his boots and tucks his socked-feet under my weighted blanket then pulls another sandwich out of the front pocket of his hoodie.

"I forgot how heavy this thing is," he says, referencing the blanket. "How do you not feel like you're suffocating under there?"

It's hard to explain to other people how much being bundled up like a burrito makes me happy, but Jamie knows me well enough that I at least don't have to start from scratch. "It's comforting. Like I'm being held."

A look of understanding washes over his face and I know

he gets it. That's the thing about Jamie. Even when there are new things he doesn't know about me, once he discovers them, they just click into place.

He never asks why. Only, what can I do?

Then his face falls. He hangs his head but I can see the grimace that takes shape. "I made you feel this way, didn't I?" he asks.

"How you acted didn't scare me," I promise, just as I did this morning at his kitchen island. That conversation feels like it happened days ago. "I just feel like you're keeping something from me. I don't want us to have secrets between us."

He stares at me in anguish, and I just know he has something he wants to say, but he doesn't. Instead, he kisses me lightly on the forehead.

"Nothing has changed, Rae. I swear it. It's you and me. You're still my best friend."

I desperately want his words to reassure me, but I can't ignore his dismissal of my concern. Something bigger is going on here, and I need to know what it is.

Being his friend means the world to me, and it used to be all I needed, but because of everything that's happened, I'm wondering for the first time what it would feel like to have more.

PART TWO:
Full Moon

Chapter Ten

JAMIE

I end up staying the night with Raegan. I hate seeing her like this. I've seen her anxiety get the best of her sometimes, but it's never been so bad that she purposely locked herself in her room and avoided my calls. I wish I could pick her up and put her in my pocket. If I could, I'd carry her with me everywhere, and there would never be a moment she didn't feel safe and secure.

This situation with Patrick has fucked her up more than I realized. Knowing he not only caused her physical harm but stressed her out to the point she doesn't even want to be outside has me livid all over again, but right now my priority isn't getting back at him. It's being here for Raegan.

All I want is to burrow myself under the covers and tuck her into my arms. Even now, when I know I shouldn't be thinking about such things, my mind wanders to what it would feel like to have her body pressed so close to mine. But I stay where I am on top of the covers. Long after she falls asleep, I'm still fighting the temptation, and after several hours I manage to wrangle it into submission.

I feel like I've only been asleep for an hour when I wake up to the sound of birds chirping outside her bedroom window.

The room is completely dark, thanks to her blackout curtains doing the utmost work at blocking out the outside world. I glance at my watch and see it's six forty in the morning. I internally groan.

Typically I don't need to get ready for work for another hour, so I rest my head back against the pillow and allow myself time to just lay here. It's been a while since I've truly rested. Between running the coffee shop, trying to keep up with basic human hygiene, and worrying about Raegan's safety every second of the day, my mind has been on overdrive. But right now, for the first time in a week, everything is quiet. So I relax.

I allow myself another ten minutes to do just that, then my brain starts whirring back to life. My first thought is to make Raegan breakfast before she goes to work. I carefully roll to my side and into a sitting position. Her bed is way less creaky than the one I've been making her sleep in at my house. Maybe I should pull the trigger and finally get a new bed frame for the guest room.

I stand from the bed just as Raegan moans grumpily and shifts positions. A smile warms my face. There are so many versions of her, and I love every one of them. The stubborn, confrontational Raegan, the overthinker, the playful and light-hearted Raegan, and the one I'm looking at now: the unguarded Raegan in her safe place. A perfect little burrito protected from the world.

It takes me thirty minutes to scramble eggs and crisp up some bacon in her mini air fryer. By the time I'm plating her meal, Raegan shuffles out of her bedroom with tired eyes and slippers the shape of cat paws. She's changed out of her clothes from yesterday and is now wearing a sweatshirt and sleep shorts.

She's clearly not planning on getting ready for work.

"Are you staying home today?" I ask gently.

She eyes the door carefully, as if avoiding full eye contact with it. She's still not ready to step back outside, and that's perfectly okay. Only this time, she won't be alone.

Instead of speaking, she slowly nods.

I hand over the plate of bacon and eggs with a side of sliced up strawberries. "Eat this, and then you can go back to bed, if you want."

She takes it from me carefully, picking up a slice of bacon to take a bite. I watch her perk up as she chews. "You always cook it perfectly."

Seeing her happy dance when she eats good food always makes me smile, but there's a satisfaction in knowing I cooked it the way she likes.

"I need to text Ethan and tell him I'm not coming in," she says quietly.

"I'll let him know," I say. From what she confided in me last night, I know having to talk to people will only make her anxiety worse. So, any pressure I can offload from her I will.

She knows what I'm doing, and the small tug at the corners of her lips only reassures me I'm doing the right thing.

"Are you going to stay out here, or do you want to go back to your room?" I ask.

She takes in the sight of her small apartment and I can see that her tense posture from yesterday has now relaxed.

"I'm okay here." She settles on the couch and turns on the tv. Meanwhile, Cleetus wanders out from some unknown hiding place to plop onto her lap. He gives me a withering stare, but Raegan pats the spot next to her for me to sit down.

I expected her to want to go back to her room and eat, so I'm taking the fact that she's in the living room as a good sign.

Expanding the perimeter of her foxhole has to mean she's feeling better.

I join her for a few minutes while she eats and we watch the first segment of a morning talk show. When she's done with her breakfast, she rests her head on my shoulder, and I have to physically tear myself from the couch when it's time for me to leave.

I grab my keys from where I left them on the counter the night before and come back to crouch in front of her. Cleetus snarls, but Raegan smacks him lightly on the butt.

I stare right into his territorial eyes and make sure he knows I'm the true predator here. Somehow the silent communication works, because he flees from Raegan's lap and darts for her bedroom, tail puffed up behind him.

Raegan looks confused. "Why can't you two just get along?"

"He just got spooked," I say, then pull her attention back to me by placing my hand on her knee. "If you need anything, you call me. Got it?" She nods. "I'm going to open the store and check on a few inventory things, then I'm going to take the rest of the day off. I'll be done around noon, so I'll bring us some lunch."

She's looking at me with a mixture of astonishment and gratitude, and there's a sharp pang in my chest. I don't like that her first instinct is to be surprised by my kindness. I know she has faith in me, but I think deep down she's somehow convinced herself that the place she's currently in is meant to be experienced alone. But she's wrong.

From this moment forward, Raegan will never again be surprised by my willingness to take care of her. The next time she needs to close herself in her room and hide under the covers, I'll be right there beside her.

I place a kiss on her forehead and this time I linger just a bit longer. I close my eyes and breathe in her scent, letting everything that is *her* fill and recharge my soul. When I pull back, she's looking up at me with bright and glossy eyes.

Suddenly, I have a strong awareness of my own heartbeat. It thuds against my chest as if to remind me it's there. I'm flooded with a warm sensation and my palms are sweaty. I have to force myself to stand up and look away from her.

"I'll be back in a few hours," I say, hoping she doesn't hear the crack in my voice. "Hang tight."

Raegan tucks into the couch and curls an arm around her middle. "See you then." She's clearly noticed me purposefully pulling away, and I want to scream that it's not what she thinks.

These small moments between us are happening more and more. Everytime she witnesses a moment of weakness from me, when my wolf manages to break the surface and attempt to seize the moment and claim her, I have to yank it back and shove it down. She probably thinks it's because I don't want her, but that couldn't be further from the truth.

The full moon is in two days, and every second that ticks by we move closer and closer to the moment I'll have no choice but to shift. Given everything that's happened, I don't see myself in a situation where I'll be able to leave Raegan's side for more than a few hours, so how the hell am I going to successfully stay gone for two days? For twelve hours I'll be in my wolf form, and shifting back is so exhausting I typically end up sleeping the entire next day.

After closing the front door behind me, I lean back against the frame and run a hand down my face. I still have thirty-six hours to figure things out, which means this is just another problem for future me to solve.

. . .

AFTER A MORNING of zero productivity at Double Double, I stop by Kiki's Cafe to order a pimento grilled cheese and extra crispy fries for Raegan. After checking out the specials menu, I order a fried green tomato BLT.

When it's ready, Brendon, Kiki's son, slides my to-go bag over the counter with a wink. The kid has only just turned eighteen yet is covered in tattoos of everything from a ketchup bottle to a koala on fire. The one time I asked about them, he said he liked having physical reminders of significant moments in his life.

I still don't get it.

"Gave you extra aioli," he tells me slyly, as if he's slipped drugs into the bag.

I shake my head and roll my eyes. "Thanks, boss."

As the bell above the door dings to signal my exit, I hear Kiki's voice over the bustling lunch crowd. "Tell Raegan we've got her back!" she shouts, a piercing edge to her banshee voice. I wince, along with several patrons while still murmuring their agreement. "That shit with legs is gonna rot for what he did!"

Being married to Sheriff Simmons, I'm sure Kiki got all the juicy details about the arrest after the fact. I've managed to avoid the gossip mill since leaving work last night, so I'm not caught up on the latest verdict. I know Twitty took Patrick to the police station with Aidan, but Shadow Hills Precinct only has two jail cells, one of which is mostly utilized as a drunk tank for Mayor Musthaven's nephew, Phillip, who gets shit-faced drunk off moonshine vapors every night and then floats out of his cell every morning.

I wonder if Patrick will be transferred to the city given his assault charges. The further away the better.

I give Kiki and the rest of the cafe a thumbs up and head back to Raegan's apartment. When I get there, she's horizontal and curled into a ball on the couch watching a cooking show.

She startles slightly when I open the door, but her shoulders relax after seeing it's me.

I hold up the take out bag from Kiki's and her eyes brighten. "Pimento grilled cheese?" she asks.

"And fries."

She jumps up from the couch and rushes to the kitchen counter where I lay out all the food, picking up the bag of fries and holding it to her cheek. "They're fresh," she says wholesomely before turning her gaze to me. "You're my hero!"

She certainly makes me feel like one.

We both agree that the fries from Kiki's are better than any fast food chain because they're double fried. That extra crisp makes all the difference, and as I watch Raegan take her first bite, I'm happy to see that something so small is able to bring her so much joy.

I spend the rest of the day by her side. We watch a marathon of one of our favorite crime dramas that's playing on TV while devouring the food I brought. After a few hours, we decide it's time for a snack, so together we playfully make tacos in her kitchen with a pack of nearly expired tortillas and whatever toppings she happens to have on hand.

Raegan uses rotisserie chicken, greek dressing, feta, and cherry tomatoes. I decide on leftover ground beef I found in a tupperware container, sprinkle cheese, and a mixture of ketchup, mustard, and mayo for the sauce.

"Why'd you have to make yours so refined?" I tease her.

She scoffs. "What's so fancy about a chicken wrap?"

I gape at her. "It's not supposed to be a wrap! The point was to make a taco out of random ingredients!"

"Your taco is not random. You basically made a cheeseburger."

"Exactly. A cheeseburger taco is awesome."

She takes a massive bite of her creation, dressing running

down her chin. "Well my Mediterranean taco is delicious," she says, mouth full.

"It's a wrap," I deadpan, but she just continues eating.

We laugh, sliding down the cabinets to sit on the floor.

She's leaning back against the bottom row of cabinets with one leg tucked in close and the other stretched across the floor. Her slippered foot taps against my thigh as I sit perpendicular to her, my long legs reaching from one side of her tiny kitchen to the other. We've finished eating, but neither of us has made a move to get up. Down here, it feels like another safe pocket for her to hide in, only this time we've made it together.

My thumb haphazardly traces circles on her calf, and as I watch, the rest of my fingers move slowly over her knee and up to her thigh, I see goosebumps raise along her flesh. She must have noticed it too, because she bends her leg, effectively pulling it from my reach.

Something is brewing beneath the surface for both of us. I know my reason for fighting it—it's clearly my wolf nature trying to stake its claim on her—but what's her reason for pulling away? The only logical explanation is that she will never see me as more than a friend. Yet when I catch her swallowing a lump in her throat, I know that can't be true. There have been signs, like the way she looked at me this morning, her eyes glimmering with a word I can't fathom.

After my first shift, I spent an extensive amount of time with the pack, learning the signs of my natural instincts and how to fight against them when in my human form. If I wanted to keep my secret, I had to hold back my aggressive nature when placed in a conflict outside of my control. And I have. For the most part.

I should have been able to keep my cool with Patrick, but every time I was confronted by him, one outlying factor changed everything: Raegan.

It was her presence that triggered my need to show dominance, to crush him under my heel and claim her as *mine*. The word echoes in the back of my mind like a mantra each time I feel the need to protect her.

Mine.

Mine.

Mine.

Even now, as I sit inches from her warm body, I want to sink my teeth into her. Leave my mark on that perfect porcelain skin so everyone who sees it knows it was me.

I close my eyes and let out a low groan.

Why now? I question the universe. *Why is all of this happening now?*

She's been in my life for fucking fifteen years, and suddenly *now* is when my wolf wants to fuck her like an animal? But it's not just lust clouding my vision. It feels like every single part of me, on a cellular level, is being pulled toward her, and there is nothing I can do to change course.

Every pack member I've asked about it over the years has said the same thing about finding my mate: I'll just know.

At the time, the notion sounded dumb as hell, like something I'd hear out of one of Raegan's smutty romance novels. But now? I can't help but think they were right. Just the thought of her not by my side sends a flash of red across my vision.

She's staring at me guiltily, and I can see the questioning look on her face as she internally reprimands herself for pulling away from my touch. So I place my hand on the top of her adorable cat paw slipper and squeeze.

I'm about to tell her what I'm feeling—that what we're both feeling is natural—but instead I blurt out something else entirely. "I want you to move in with me."

Chapter Eleven

RAEGAN

I wish I could say I wasn't shocked by Jamie's confession, but I am. He offers for me to move in with him every time my lease is up, but he's never flat out asked me because it's what he wants.

There are several reasons why I continue to turn him down: one being my pride and another being I love my apartment no matter how expensive it is. But now I'm wondering if something new should be added to the list.

Touches from Jamie no longer just comfort me. They send a shiver down my spine. Dismissing the occasional lustful thought has been easy while still having space from one another, but if I moved in with him, it would be near impossible to ignore the little moments between us that keep happening more and more.

I stare at him blankly for several seconds, then draw a breath and release it heavily. "Jamie–"

"Don't," he cuts me off. "I've already heard every one of your excuses, and none of them are good enough." I try to interject, but he stops me. "Your lease with Mavis is up in a little over a week. Either you stay here, barely making it paycheck to paycheck and continuing to stress yourself out for no reason—" I open my mouth. "Or," he overstates, "you come live with me, rent free, and save some money. Plus you'll get plenty of one-on-one time with your best friend."

That's exactly what I'm afraid of.

I cross my arms and keep my eyes trained on the floor in front of me.

"Come on," he practically begs. "Besides your pride, what's holding you back?"

I lift my head to give him a pointed look, as if to say 'you know exactly what's holding me back.' It's that pull toward one another that we've been feeling but are too afraid to talk about.

"Rae, what is it?"

My hand flutters to my neck. I snuck a peek at myself in the mirror this morning, too afraid to look for more than a second. Even so, I managed to catch the now purple bruise blooming at the base of my throat.

Instead of voicing my true concern, I ask, "What about Cleetus? We're a package deal." We both look to my bedroom door, slightly ajar from where he slipped inside moments ago.

As much as Jamie probably loathes the idea of my cat prancing around his condo and scratching the shit out of his furniture, he also knows how much of a comfort Cleetus is to me. He's been my emotional support animal for the past seven years.

"I know you two can't be separated. He's your best friend."

I chuckle. "*You're* my best friend."

"Sometimes I wonder," he jokes. "Besides, he's the one cuddling with you in bed every night."

The comment strikes me right in my gut, and I feel those pesky butterflies making their move again. My eyes must be bulging from their sockets, because the look on his face makes me think he wishes he could take it back.

Neither one of us address the comment, instead we both laugh it off.

"If you're sure you're okay with it...but I also come with a lot of books. And kitchen decor." I gesture to my lemon themed kitchen, complete with lemon hand towels and oven mitts, a giant lemon fruit bowl, lemon glasses and bowls, and a lemon timer. That's not even half of it.

"Yes, Rae. I will gladly take your books and all your lemon shit."

I gasp dramatically. "Jamie Trent! My lemon decor is not shit!"

He chuckles. "Okay, lemon."

"Oh no, is that going to be my nickname from now on?"

"Maybe." He cocks his head, visibly rolling the name over in his head. "It's cute."

I'm a sucker for a romance book in which the love interest gives the main character a nickname. I try to imagine him calling me lemon in a non-cute way, perhaps when he's hovering over me, my legs spread...

Too far, Raegan.

When I don't respond, he nudges me playfully. "Well? What do you say? Are you moving in with me?" It's hard to focus on Jamie's sincere expression with my vision currently clouded with lust. He takes my silence as hesitation, so he back-tracks a little. "We'll just see how it goes. If it doesn't work out, I'll help you find a new place. I promise. Just let me do this for you."

It's sweet that he always considers my comfort first, but I think I'm done fighting against what I've secretly wanted for a long time now. Sure, I might be opening myself to be crushed, but who's to say I can't enjoy some close proximity with him while I can?

I nod and smile, confirming my choice. "Okay."

I want to be near him. I want to feel safe and secure, and I know Jamie is the best person to do that.

HE STAYS with me again that night, and I fall asleep easily knowing he's next to me. Even without touching him, his presence is enough to soothe any anxious feelings still burrowing into the back of my mind.

There's no doubt now that there's something different about the way I'm drawn to him. It isn't just a history of friendship and trust, or the feeling of safety from being around someone who knows me better than anyone else.

Somewhere deep in my chest, it feels like imaginary hands are reaching out toward him, begging to pull us closer. It's raw and primal, and the further I wade into these new feelings, the more consuming it feels.

It sounds impossible, but I have never needed something as much as I need to be close to him. Just having him in my sights is a powerful thing.

As I drift off listening to the sound of his steady breathing, I wonder if it's possible for humans to have soulmates.

If so, I'm pretty sure he's mine.

Chapter Twelve

RAEGAN

I'm the first to wake on Wednesday morning. It's nine thirty, and typically Jamie would already be drinking a cup of coffee and almost done making breakfast by now. Yet, when I look behind me, I find him still sound asleep in my bed.

His left arm is draped haphazardly across his forehead, mouth gaping. I silently laugh and grab his forearm to reposition it at his side, but when I do, I feel the scorching temperature of his skin. I touch his forehead and confirm it's burning up.

Reaching over to dig in my nightstand, I pull out an electronic thermometer. I pull the trigger and wait for it to read. With a beep, the screen shows 101.3.

"Shit," I whisper.

I try to rouse him awake by rubbing his shoulder, but he only groans and rolls over to face the window. With his back facing me, I feel a wave of heat coming off his body.

"Jamie, I think you're sick."

He stiffens, clearly awake, and I spy his hand on the other side of the bed creating a fist in the sheets.

This time my voice quivers. "Jamie?"

He bolts upright and stretches dramatically. "That was the best sleep of my life," he says, totally casual.

"Jamie," I say his name again but more forcefully to grab his attention, "your temperature is high. Do you feel okay?"

He turns to face me with a bright smile and absolutely no sign of discomfort. "I'm fine. My temp runs naturally high."

"Over a hundred is natural?"

His smile falters for just a second but immediately slips back into place. "I probably caught a cold or something," he suggests. "Remember, Casey was coughing at work the other day?"

I definitely don't remember that but I nod emphatically anyway, just to set both him and myself at ease. Only it's not working on my end.

"So listen," he says, standing to grab his jacket and his boots, "I took off today because I've got some errands to run. I probably won't be by again until tomorrow. Will you be alright?"

He's asking if I'm capable of being by myself for the next twenty-four hours, and though I know he doesn't mean it this way, it feels like pity.

I take a moment to assess my current mental state and try to imagine myself walking out the front door and down the steps, feeling fresh air on my skin, and knowing the entire world is open before me.

Miraculously, I don't flinch.

"I'm better now," I tell him, and it feels true.

I don't think going back to my normal routine will send me into a panic spiral. It's time I faced the outside again: aka the town and all their questions. Ethan texted me last night telling me I could take off the rest of the week. I was surprised by his generosity, given he's not one for taking a mental health day, but most likely he's just waiting for the drama to die down.

I try to shape the look on my face into something resembling confidence, but it's been a minute since I've felt that particular feeling. Without any other questions, Jamie nods and accepts my answer. Either I managed to pass his inspection with flying colors, or he just ignored any cracks in my facade. I'm beginning to think it's the latter.

He hurriedly grabs the rest of his things, and before heading out the door, he leans in to brush a kiss to my cheek. Though it's less than a second, I feel him lingering to feel the press of my skin against his. I relish the sensation and tuck it away in the back of my mind for later use. In case I need the memory as a life raft in another episode of panic.

"I'll be back tomorrow," he promises.

I hear the sincerity in the tone of his voice, and I know he means it. Whatever it is that's driving him away right now, he won't let it keep him from me for long.

The door closes gently and I listen for the click of the handle as it settles in place. The moment he's gone, I exhale the breath I'd been hoarding in my chest.

"You're fine," I tell myself out loud. "Everything is fine."

IT TAKES me longer than usual to get myself ready. Instead of the quick ten minute shower I tend to stick to, I linger under the warm water for twenty minutes. I don't bother drying or styling my hair, only glaze the strands with leave-in conditioner to prevent frizz and let nature take its course.

I know I'm delaying the inevitable when it takes me almost thirty minutes to pick out my outfit. I've never put so much thought into what I'm wearing before, but internally I know it's a stall tactic. Eventually, I decide to wear my favorite pair of millennial skinny jeans and one of my seasonal transition sweaters. It's made from a deep maroon material that's super soft and will help usher in the Autumn spirit, but it's thin enough that I won't melt in the afternoon heat. I finish off the ensemble with an old pair of low top Chucks. The outfit is simple, but it's comfortable—something I really need right now.

Standing in front of the mirror, I take in my appearance. Not the outfit or the still damp hair, but my face. I see the lines of worry around my brow and the corners of my mouth. My skin is dry and patchy from skipping my nightly moisturizer twice in a row. Yet there's no part of me that cares.

The purple marks on my neck are more pronounced than ever, but I can't bring myself to do anything to cover them. As much as I wish I could hide away from what happened, I don't want to negate the seriousness of what Patrick did. Part of me wants everyone to see the bruise, and as I take a deep breath and plaster a smile on my face, that part of me wins. The mirror knows the gesture is fake, but hopefully no one else will.

I make sure Cleetus is fed and clean out his litter box that I've neglected for three days. He thanks me by rubbing against my legs and purring loudly.

"I'm sorry, sweet boy," I apologize, crouching down to scratch his chin the way he likes. "I had a rough few days."

He places a paw on my knee and I know this means he's accepted.

"If Jamie hadn't been here, you would take care of me, wouldn't you?" He bumps his head against my thigh. "You always do."

I grab either side of his face and kiss his forehead emphatically before grabbing my bag and heading out. The door closes behind me and I wait momentarily for the expanse of hallway to overwhelm me, but instead I find myself eager to start my day. This is the best sign I could hope for.

Giving myself little things to look forward to has always been a great tool for motivation. And now, as I venture slowly back to the simulation of my old self, I try to give myself a reward.

If I make it into town, I'll go straight to Kiki's and get a butter pecan iced coffee.

I'm not purposefully avoiding Double Double—Jamie isn't working today anyway, and Kiki makes the better holiday drinks since Jamie never likes to go "cutesy" with his menu. Besides the fall themed beverages he's forced to serve at the Founding Festival, the most spirited coffee he's ever offered was the year he allowed one of his part-time baristas to get creative with the cafe lattes at Christmas. She created a little reindeer with the foam, and the town ate them up that holiday season.

Right now, I'm craving the feel of autumn in the air, and as I step out onto the staircase that leads down to the parking lot, I'm ecstatic to feel a crisp breeze blow across my face. It's a bit chilly with my wet hair, but every muscle in my body relaxes at the touch of cool air, and instead of a push to go back inside, I feel a pull to venture further.

On the ride into town, I roll down my windows. I'll probably end up with that fake cold Jamie has, but I can't bring myself to care. Instead, I allow the chill to seep into my bones, waking me up from my two day hibernation.

As I turn onto Main Street, I spy the many dots of orange in every window and outside every door. The Founding Day Festival is two weeks away, and though everyone is hustling to get things in order, the sight of my home town dressed to the nines ushers in a breath of relief that immediately relaxes my shoulders.

I park in my usual spot outside of Kiki's and glance over at

Double Double across the street. I can see through the decorless windows that Layton, the assistant manager, is running the register. Looks like Jamie was telling the truth about being off today. I hate that it was instinct to check, and afraid my distrust is only going to grow the more he keeps hiding from me.

Inside the cafe, I'm greeted first by Kiki's sister, Kendra, as she sits at the bar top waiting for her breakfast sandwich to-go. Being close in age, the redheaded sisters almost look like twins, but their personalities set them entirely apart. Besides Kendra having shorter hair, I've identified a few key differences between the two. Kendra has a dimple on the left side of her cheek when she smiles, and Kiki tends to have an indignant expression on her face at all times, her eyebrows are tilted in a perpetual furrow. She's also the more outspoken of the two. Kendra's aura gives off kind and bubbly energy, while Kiki's, kind as it may be, makes people take a step back.

Kendra lets out a banshee shriek when she sees me and nearly falls off her stool. She stumbles and falls into an embrace around my torso. My ears are still ringing when she pulls back to look at me.

"I'm so glad to see you," she cries with joy. "Honey, where have you been? When I heard what happened, I wanted to march on over to the police station and smack that hooligan myself for what he did to you!" She makes an obvious effort to avoid looking at my neck as she says this.

I knew people would start asking questions the minute I showed my face back in town, but I at least hoped to get a coffee first. Kendra's doting, motherly spirit doesn't concern me though. I know she means well and only wants to check on me.

"Thank you, Kendra," I placate. "I'm just grateful he's gone."

She *humphs* and nods curtly. "Sit down, sweetheart. Get yourself a coffee."

"Precisely my plan."

Though she's only ten years older than me, Kendra has always felt like a motherly figure. My mother isn't a bad mother, but she's never been quite as doting as Kendra. Though she cares for me, I believe my mother's first priority will always be the coven, and I can't blame her for that. Especially given I don't have magic. Why would she waste time on me when witches under her supervision need her more?

I take in Kendra's outfit and fawn over her creativity. She's wearing a black jumpsuit with golden suns and moons creating a pattern across the fabric, and accented with gold eyeliner to match. To tie it all together, she's added a red patchwork cardigan over top for a pop of color.

"You're always so stylish," I compliment her. "And autumn is your best time of year."

"I wholeheartedly agree." She twirls on the spot before sitting back down, and I hear a whoop from the back corner.

"Thanks, Maurice!" Kendra takes a dramatic bow.

I'm pretty sure the bar owner has had the hots for her since they were in school together.

The cook behind the open window snaps his fingers appraisingly, but then Kiki steps out from the kitchen, the two-way doors swinging wildly in her wake.

"Kenny, why are you shouting so early in the morning?" the older sister demands.

Kendra freezes in place and looks abashed. She brushes over her cardigan as if flattening invisible wrinkles then plops back on the stool beside me. Meanwhile, I'm fighting to hide an enormous grin.

Kiki stomps over to where Kendra and I are sitting at the counter with a scowl on her face. "Why are you disruptin' my customers?" Her straight red hair is pulled up into a bun and covered with a hairnet, loose strands protruding from every opening.

Kendra looks offended. "I wasn't *disruptin'* anybody."

"We were just admiring her fashion sense, Kiki," I say, attempting to ease the tension.

The disgruntled sister turns to me and her scowl fades. "Raegan, you're back."

I didn't realize not showing my face in town for two days would result in everyone thinking I left, but I guess that goes to show how upsetting the routine of a small town can throw everyone off kilter.

"I decided to take a vacation," I tell her, and everyone in earshot. The entire cafe has quieted enough that they clearly want to hear the conversation. Both sisters' eyes roam over my throat, looking for the bruise, but my hair is covering most of it from sight. "I'm fine," I add. "Just glad it's over."

Kiki gives me a pitying grin, and I can tell she wants to say more, but unlike Kendra, she keeps her comments to herself. "Alright!" she barks, clapping her hands to grab everyone's attention. "Everyone back to your breakfast! This ain't a soap opera!" The murmur of individual conversations fills the air, and just like that, the cafe resumes order.

Kendra scoots her stool closer and leans in. Apparently she isn't done prying. "I haven't seen Jamie around much either," she suggests. "Is he with you?"

"Not right now, but we umm–just hung out at my place until things died down."

Her eyebrows arch. "He stayed with you?"

I hesitate. "Yeah, he just wanted to make sure I was okay."

Now her playful curiosity turns to concern. "Oh sweetheart," her voice steady with a sudden awareness. "Of course. I should have known what happened would trigger a panic attack."

Hearing it from her makes me cringe. Like I'm a patient in need of a padded room. Kendra is the only other person who has witnessed one of my episodes, but still, she doesn't truly understand how bad it can get.

I had been extremely stressed at work one day, and Kendra happened to be browsing the shelves. A disagreement with a customer led to me hyperventilating behind the counter, so Kendra pulled me aside and dragged us to the back corner of the store. In the very last row of books, beneath the dusty sign saying ESSAYS AND POETRY, I allowed myself five minutes to panic, and Kendra was right there the entire time holding my hand. She told me she suffered from panic attacks as a teenager, but that the anxiety never really goes away. You just learn to manage it.

Her advice was enough to clear my head, and I went back to work. Ever since then, she's taken the time to check in, asking about my mental health. I appreciate it, but it only reminds me that I'm a basket case.

A basket case that Jamie is now forced to carry.

I know he said he would be busy today, but I'm suddenly overwhelmed with the need to see him. The way we parted this morning still doesn't sit right with me, and I think it's time I start asking questions, instead of worrying myself into another episode.

Something was clearly wrong with him when I took his temperature. No one's temp naturally runs that high. However, Jamie *is* the type of person to ignore symptoms when it comes to being sick, especially if he's busy with something important.

The week of Double Double's grand opening, he came down with strep throat, but never told anyone until he was in so much pain he couldn't talk. I had to drag him to the clinic so they could load him up on antibiotics and pump him full of fluids. He still managed to be there on opening day, greeting everyone at the door with his boyish grin.

I love that grin.

"I'm glad he was there," Kendra says, pulling me from my daydreaming. "I swear that boy never leaves your side. You're like two peas in a pod."

I've heard the sentiment many times. Everyone in town knows how close we are.

"He certainly took it personally when that man put his hands on you," she continues, as if we're gossiping. "From what I heard, Jamie looked possessed. Reminds me of when his uncle first met Paloma. He helped her leave a pretty nasty relationship, and after that, they were inseparable. I tell you what, I have never seen anyone more livid than a werewolf protecting their mate." She cocks her head, but I'm no longer listening to anything she's saying. "As a matter of fact..."

Suddenly all of Jamie's odd behavior starts flashing like a slideshow in my mind. His severe aggression toward Patrick, the overly attentive nature he's shown me, and now suddenly disappearing after being glued to my side for days. It all lines up a little too perfectly.

It's as if there's a full moon making him act so out of character.

My heart skips a beat. I hurriedly grab my bag from the hook beneath the counter and dig for my phone. Kendra is trying to ask me something, but I don't have the mental capacity to answer her. Right now my mind is focused on one thing: opening my calendar app. As I click to the current week and select today's date, I spy the little moon graphic in the corner of the box.

No flippin' way.

I've known Jamie since high school. If he was a werewolf, there would have been signs. He would have told me.

Would he?

Had I somehow given him a reason not to trust me with such a profound part of himself? And not just me, but the entire town. The whole point of Shadow Hills' founding was to provide a safe place for paranormals. Why in the world would Jamie choose to keep his nature a secret in the one place that would truly accept him?

I stand up and rush to the door, appetite forgotten.

"Where you goin'?" Kendra asks. "You haven't ordered yet!"

"I just remembered I need to check on something." I'm already halfway outside when I call back to her. "I still want to come by and see those kittens!"

I see her dumbfounded expression through the window as I pass but don't stop. I race across the street to Double Double, praying someone knows where Jamie is.

Chapter Thirteen

RAEGAN

I know Jamie won't be there, but perhaps his assistant manager will know what errands he's meant to run today.

The dim and moody atmosphere of the coffee shop is a stark difference to Kiki's bright and bustling cafe. I love the style Jamie chose for his business, but I have to admit, it does bring down the mood a bit after coming from Kiki's. Maybe that's what he meant to achieve. When someone enters Double Double, they are escaping the chaos of the outside world and taking refuge among a quiet, slow paced setting.

I guess no one is in need of escape today, because the place is completely empty, save for Casey balancing empty coffee cups on top of each other behind the counter. They startle when I walk toward them and have to catch the falling cups as they tumble from their makeshift tower.

I'm about to ask if they've spoken to Jamie yet today, but then Layton comes out from the back carrying a box of coffee grounds. I wave hello and he greets me with an open mouthed smile. His long dreads cascade down his back and just barely skim his waist as he bends to place the box on the floor to unpack.

His golden eyes find mine. "Jamie isn't here today," he says, assuming correctly who I'm looking for. Only I already knew that.

"Oh, I know." I wave the comment away with my hand, pretending I haven't just realized something life changing about my best friend. "He told me he wasn't working today, but that he had errands to run. Did he need to do a supply pick up?"

Both Layton and I glance down at the full box of ground coffee and fresh beans he just brought from the storeroom. Jamie locally sources his coffee from a vendor just outside of town, and clearly they were fully stocked.

Layton forces a chuckle. "No, we did that last week." He looks me up and down, searching for any sign that something might be amiss. "Is everything alright?"

I nod emphatically. "Yeah, fine. I just forgot where he said he was going today and I need to track him down for something. No biggie." I fake a laugh and shrug my shoulders casually. "See you around."

I wave goodbye and turn for the door, but he offers one more comment that has me stopping.

"He didn't look too good," Layton suggests. "Did he not tell you he was sick?"

I catch Casey staring at me from the corner of my eye.

"Right," I force out quickly. "That's why I'm looking for him." I fake a laugh and roll my eyes. "He's always working and never taking care of himself, am I right?"

Layton gives me a nervous laugh. He can probably tell there's something bigger going on here, but he's too polite to insert himself into our private business.

"He mentioned that Fabio-looking vampire before he left. Maybe he went there for some reason?"

There were only two resident vampires in Shadow Hills: the two hundred year old teenager who never left his property in the woods, and Aidan, the white haired forever thirty-something specimen who lived beneath the movie theater.

As a good friend of Jamie's, Aidan frequents Double Double almost every morning. I haven't spoken to him much, but after his heroic act of stopping Patrick from choking me to death, perhaps I ought to pay him a visit. At least to thank him for saving my life.

I give Layton my appreciation and head the opposite direction down Main, aiming for the movie theater at the very end of the street. I pass the bookstore, my and Jamie's favorite sushi restaurant, and the local deli. The theater appears at the corner of East and Main, its bright red awning and marquee signaling the building like a beacon. Currently the letters read MONSTER MOVIE WEEKEND THIS SAT & SUN!

I'm shocked to see there's something new playing, given the same 80s teen movie has been playing for months. No one's ever been able to complain, because no one can figure out who the owner is. We know it's definitely someone in town, but they've chosen to keep their identity a secret for whatever reason.

To the right of the entrance is a railing that leads to a set of descending steps. The original owner, Maurice who now owns Bones, the only bar in town, decided instead of building his apartment above the business he would create an underground living space to avoid the noise. Now he has his own cabin in the woods, only a few miles past the wolf pack territory.

Suddenly reminded of why I'm here, I grab the large bronze knocker resembling a gargoyle and bang the handle against the door three times. Regardless of how hard I knock, I assume a vampire would hear me. And just like that, less than a second after letting go, the door swings open.

Layton's Fabio description of Aidan really was quite accurate. His shoulder length white hair is perfectly layered and has enough volume to make me jealous. His deep-set, piercing blue eyes sit slightly too close together, yet remain perfectly symmetrical with the rest of his features. His wide nose leads down to a set of pursed thin lips and a rounded jaw, and his high forehead remains unwrinkled while holding a curious expression.

After realizing who the visitor is, he relaxes. "Raegan." He says my name softly, as if trying not to spook me.

"Hi!" I greet him animatedly, adding an actual wave, and Aidan looks a bit scared.

You're overselling it.

"Hey," I try again, "so, this is odd, but would you happen to know where Jamie is?"

Aidan's already pale skin turns ashen as he lifts his head and searches the sky. "He hasn't spoken to you?"

"I saw him this morning, but..." Part of me wants to tell him the truth of why I'm worried. At least he could tell me if I'm overreacting.

Aidan relents and steps aside, gesturing for me to come in. I step over the threshold and am welcomed by an enormous chandelier hanging only a few feet above my head. It hovers even closer above Aidan as he steps beneath it.

"The ceilings are low," he says, "but I still have standards."

I find it hilarious he felt the need to explain. The space is much larger than I thought it would be. Besides the low ceilings, I would never be able to tell I was below ground.

Aidan's home gives off the same vibe as Double Double's dark and moody aesthetic, only the decor here has a modern gothic twist. The walls are gray and dark, and dramatic furniture fills the room. There's a baroque-inspired coffee table with ornate legs in the middle of a large woven area rug, surrounded by a black velvet lounge and a deep red brocade armchair. An enormous fireplace sits parallel to the entryway that I'm pretty sure is taller than me. I never visited when Maurice lived here, but I'm guessing it looked a lot different than this.

I take a seat on the velvet couch and sink back into a set of fringe pillows. Aidan remains standing, but offers to make tea. I shake my head.

"He didn't tell you where he was going today?" Aidan asks.

I swallow a lump in my throat. "Well, he told me he was running errands, and that I wouldn't see him again until tomorrow." I wipe my sweaty palms down my jeans. "It's really not a big deal, I was just wondering if he was here, or maybe...I dunno."

Aidan takes in my defeated sigh with a stoic posture. It's hard to decipher what he's feeling when he shows so little emotion on his face. Most of the time his expression rests in an award-winning poker face, giving absolutely nothing away. However, my concern about Jamie has caught him off guard, and the slightest tightening of his jaw reveals his worry.

I don't know why, but something makes me just blurt out the question that's been on my mind since leaving the cafe. "Has Jamie ever told you anything about himself? Something he might not want others to know."

Aidan gives me a pointed look, but I hold my chest high. There's no turning back now. For a moment, he looks as if he wants to slap himself, or possibly me, across the face.

Have I opened a can of worms?

"How has he been acting?" Aidan asks as he takes a seat in the armchair. He crosses his legs and folds his hands gracefully in his lap. It's as if he knows I've seen Jamie act out of character, but he's waiting for me to say it.

My hand absentmindedly finds the bruise on my neck

again. The physical reminder takes me back to how I felt the day it happened.

"He's been really angry lately," I admit. "Not at me, but...he seems to get enraged by anything that threatens me." Aidan nods but waits for me to continue. "And he's been, well...there's this pull I keep feeling between us, but maybe it's just me."

"A pull?" Aidan clarifies.

"That's what it feels like. There's something drawing me to him more than usual. Ever since he first confronted Patrick and told him to never come near me again, I've had this deep need to be near him. I think he feels it too." Aidan nods thoughtfully. "But this morning, he left so quickly, like he couldn't get away fast enough."

Aidan lifts his brows and waits for me to put together the pieces myself, but apparently I'm too dumb to do that. "Raegan," he starts with a slightly annoyed tone, "do you know what tonight is?"

I don't hesitate. "The full moon." I blow out a noisy breath. "B-but I would know," I sputter. "It happens every month. How could I miss something like that?"

We're dancing around the subject, but I know we're talking about the same thing.

"Have you ever spent this much consecutive time together before?"

I don't answer.

Aidan doesn't meet my eyes. He lowers his chin and lets out a long, low sigh of defeat. Whatever he's been holding back, he's choosing to let it go.

"I'm only telling you this because he should have told you himself, a long time ago," he says. "I already know you've figured out what he is, but you need to know this too. I think you're his mate. I'm pretty sure he knows, but hasn't accepted it yet. And I think you know, too."

I shake my head honestly, but inwardly I'm still in denial. "Why now?" I demand, as if Aidan holds all the answers. "After all these years, why am I only seeing the signs now?"

"You said it started when Patrick threatened you," he reiterates. "To me, it sounds like a fear for your safety is what triggered the bond to awaken within you both."

I'm dumbfounded. I try my hardest to think back to every full moon we've spent together, but after going back just a few months in my head, I realize we haven't. Either by happenstance or on purpose, Jamie and I have never been in the same room together during a full moon. Does that mean he's been going to the woods to shift on his own?

"Do the others know about him?"

I feel like I'm prying into something I shouldn't be, yet I feel like Aidan is the one to give me the answers I want when no one else can.

"They do," he confirms.

"How long?"

"For as long as he's lived in Shadow Hills, I believe."

My stomach is in knots. This is huge. After all this time, I thought Jamie and I were closer than this—close enough that we could tell each other everything—but he kept this from me, the biggest secret of all.

I don't have any more questions for Aidan. I decide I've heard enough.

I get up to leave but Aidan stops me.

"Wait." He grabs my arm carefully, and I feel the cool touch of his fingers bringing goose bumps to my skin. It's nowhere near the same feeling as when Jamie touches me. The shiver I feel from him is all desire, while Aidan's cold touch makes me want to yank my arm away.

He pulls back and apologizes. "Are you going where I think you are?"

"If he needs to shift, I assume he'll be with the others. So, yes. That's exactly where I'm going."

"I don't think it's a good idea to show up at a werewolf camp unannounced with a full moon approaching in less than twelve hours, Raegan."

Aidan's warning rushes out harshly, but I barely take it in.

"If you're right about me being his mate, they can't hurt me. Isn't that how it works?"

He steps back, dipping his head to concede. "I hope that's true. Wolves can be vicious under a full moon. They don't think like their human selves. Everything they do is about dominance and fighting for the natural order of their pack."

"I'll be fine. Thank you, Aidan." I place my hand on his shoulder. I can still feel the chill through the fabric of his shirt, but it's not nearly as cold as touching bare flesh. "Not just for this, but for saving me the other day. If you hadn't shown up when you did, I would be far worse for wear."

He eyes my throat one last time and swallows thickly. "You're welcome."

I've never been to the pack's campground before, but I have a general idea of where it's located. Otherwise, I'll just have to trust that pull inside me to lead the way.

Chapter Fourteen

JAMIE

By the time I reach camp, I've already sweat through two pairs of clothes. My first stop was to open the coffee shop and make sure everything was squared away for the next few days. Typically it takes a day of sleep to recover after a shift, but as much as I've been fighting this one off, I need to allow for a longer recoup.

I waited impatiently for Layton to show an hour after opening and asked if he was comfortable running the store alone for the next few days. I knew he would be, but I needed the verbal confirmation from him that he could handle it.

Layton has been a great assistant manager since I hired him two years ago. Eventually, my goal is to make him the lead and hire another assistant so I can take more time away from the store. Layton is patient with all the customers, incredibly organized, and a stickler for details. It's why he called out my sweaty appearance as soon as he saw me. I waved it off as an oncoming flu, which also worked as a great excuse for why I wouldn't be at the store. Leaving him to run the shop, I went to my office to change into something less sticky.

At this point my temperature was so high I could probably fry an egg on my forehead. The longer werewolves fight the urge to shift, the more our bodies fight against our will. Eventually, when the moon is high enough in the sky that its light illuminates my clammy skin, I won't have a choice. No matter how much I try to delay the inevitable, the moon has the final say. That's why I had to get out of town before that happened.

But there was one more stop I had to make before that could happen. If I couldn't be with Raegan to protect her, I needed someone else to watch over her. My rational mind knows that Patrick is currently sitting in a jail cell and out of Raegan's reach, but the irrational wolf inside keeps reminding me that anything could happen. What if he tries to break out and kidnap her? What if he has friends? Someone I don't know about to do his dirty work.

Both sides of my brain volley the possibilities back and forth to the point that I can't think straight. So just to be safe, I make a quick stop by Aidan's apartment and ask him to keep his eyes on Raegan while I'm gone. Though he agreed, that didn't dissuade him from giving me a ten minute lecture on why I should have told her about all of this sooner.

Knowing Raegan would be carefully watched over gave me a mild respite, but what truly makes my tense muscles finally relax is stepping onto werewolf territory.

Now that I can see the open expanse of woods in front of me, it's like someone has opened a window in my head and let my thoughts finally breath fresh air. The smell of damp soil and maple trees calms my racing mind, and my body finally starts to relax.

Only I'm still sweating.

No longer where anyone else can see me, I strip off my shirt and rejoice at the feel of October wind whipping against my skin. Autumn is my favorite time of year. Something about the transition of seasons makes shifting so much more freeing than when it takes place in the dead of cold or the extreme heat of summer. That in-between shift of summer to winter, or vice versa, brings a semblance of relativity with our nature and nature itself. We are both changing, ushering in a new season of life.

I close my eyes and feel the pin prick of a drizzle nip my nose and cheeks. The morning has been overcast, so the chance of rain is high, but it only makes my wolf more eager to run wild. I'm about to take off the rest of my clothes and get ready to let go when I hear footsteps approaching. Human footsteps.

Rhett, our alpha and leader of the Shadow Hills pack, steps out from behind a giant Maple and gives me a warning glare. "You're testing my patience, boy."

Rhett is in his fifties, but is in incredible shape with a towering presence. He's a good six inches taller than my five foot ten frame, and his permanent scowl framed by a bright red beard tends to keep anyone from getting too close. That's the version of Rhett most see, but I've been lucky enough to see the softer, more gentle side of him.

Not the wolf, but the man.

My uncle.

He approaches me with steady strides, flattening the fallen leaves in his path with a foreboding crunch. He looks like a warrior on the battlefield breaking the bones of his enemies as they fall beneath him. His long auburn hair is pulled back into a low ponytail, and he's wearing one of those leather bomber jackets with fur around the collar. He's the stereotypical gruff outdoorsman, only he doesn't own a motorcycle, or anything in plaid.

"Jamie." Uncle Rhett greets me with an extended hand and an open mouthed smile too big for his face, having left his rough exterior behind. "I thought for sure you'd show up at the last minute with your tail already sprouting from your behind."

I snort and take his hand firmly. He pulls me into a tight embrace and pats my back. "You stay away for too long, nephew. You should visit more. The pack howls for you on cold nights."

"No they don't."

It might sound like a joke, but I know there's some truth to what Rhett is saying. When I am separated from my pack for too long, it feels as if I've gone too long without eating. Their presence means nourishment.

I've heard it's similar to being without your mate. However, that feels more like a wound that won't heal until you can touch them again. Lately, I've begun questioning what precisely that wound feels like, because ever since my first encounter with Patrick, being away from Raegan makes me feel...uneasy. It's not painful, just a dull and constant ache. But I can't deny that it's grown in intensity. I'm afraid after I shift, that wound might grow a bit bigger.

Though I'm happy to be with my pack again and finally have the opportunity to let my body take over my racing mind, I admit I have another motive for being here.

Rhett has been mated to his wife Paloma for thirty years. If there's anyone I can ask about what it's like, it would be him. Despite my need to have that conversation, I was hoping to get the shift out of my system before running into any more werewolves in my human form. Besides my closest brothers, the rest of the pack isn't as accepting about my constant back and forth. They consider me to be a rogue wolf, given I don't live at the camp.

Even though I've lived with my wolf over half my life, part of me still hasn't accepted what I am. I fear the loss of control every month, even though I know to expect it, and being around my pack would only insight the need to shift more often.

"Come on," Rhett says. "Let me enjoy the time I've got with you before you run back to that little coffee business of yours."

I give him an indignant expression. "I thought you liked my coffee business. And I broke even in the first year, thank you very much."

"I know that." His boisterous laugh echoes among the trees. "I just like hearing you defend it so proudly." He pats my back again as we walk side by side deeper under the canopy of red and yellow leaves.

As we enter the camp, we're greeted by several young omegas running around in their wolf forms. Rhett clicks his tongue and scolds them for being so close to the perimeter. They skirt off with their little tails tucked, and the sight of them being so disciplined makes my chest tighten. Is that how I would have been if I'd grown up in the pack?

As a young teenager, I never knew how my parents really felt about paranormals. I knew they existed, and I knew about Shadow Hills and the other towns built for them to live in around the country, but they weren't talked about in my family or friend circles. After the ordinance declaring paranormals have separate land and freedom from human jurisdiction, there was a mass exodus of all paranormals from the major cities to their new small towns. After that, it was like they no longer existed.

It wasn't until I first showed signs of shifting that I learned there were other werewolves in our family. My mother immediately pulled me from public school and moved us to Shadow Hills, fearing I would face bullying and judgment from the other kids. While there isn't anything in the law that states paranormals can't live among other humans, it's pretty clearly implied that those small towns were created for a reason. Paranormals are free, but only if they live where humans tell them too.

My mom was the one to introduce me to her brother, Uncle Rhett, for the first time. He and my grandfather were the last two members of our family to have the werewolf gene. I felt such solace standing in front of someone who could truly understand what I was going through, but when Rhett offered for me to come live with the pack, I quickly said no, fearing what that would mean for me.

I was already so afraid of the changes happening to me, I desperately needed at least one thing to stay the same. So I chose to stay with my parents. During the day, I visited the pack and learned everything I needed to know about being a werewolf, and at night, I went home to my own bed and maintained some semblance of normalcy.

Some kids weren't so lucky to have parents like mine. I'd heard of young werewolves who were forced out by their families, forced to leave home and having to find packs on their own. Those kids had nothing, while I at least had a choice.

Sometimes I feel guilty for taking it for granted, knowing those without a pack would give anything to have one, but I reminded myself that this was what I needed to stay sane. As a confused teenager, I wasn't ready to give up complete control to something I didn't understand.

I'm still not.

Rhett and I pass the first cluster of mobile homes and RVs with flat tires lined against a copse of trees. There are enough for each family to have one to themselves, and there are at least twenty different families I know of that live here. The pack has been here since Shadow Hills was founded, and over the years more families have found their way to the camp.

"There he is!" a voice calls out from a small garden of vegetables. Then Clay's buzzed head pops up from behind a vine of tomatoes and gives me a shit-eating grin. "Where the hell have you been?"

"Running my business," I answer. "I haven't seen your face come by lately."

"Dude, I know." He stumbles mid stride as he steps over the small fence lining the garden. "Kyra just had the baby!" He opens his arms wide and slams into me with an aggressive hug. "I'm a dad!"

His joy is so pure, I can practically feel it radiating off him. Clay was one of the first friends I made here at the camp, and every time I see him I feel a pang of guilt for not spending more time with him.

"That's amazing, man. Congrats. I wanna see them before I go."

Clay pulls back and his joyous grin turns bitter. "You never stay long enough," he confesses, and his words are like a vise around my heart.

Despite the exhilaration I feel every time I step onto werewolf soil, the moment I shift back to my human self, I feel the itch to return home. Only this time there's something else pulling me back to Shadow Hills.

Yet again I feel that pull to get back to Raegan, but for some reason, she doesn't feel as far away as she should.

I look around at my fellow werewolves and it occurs to me that we're all still in human form. "Why haven't you all shifted yet?" I always wait until the last possible second, but typically by sunrise on the day of a full moon, the rest of the pack is already bounding through the woods.

"We've been waiting on you, brother." Clay says, looking to Rhett for confirmation.

Rhett nods and then looks at me. His eyes give the impression he wants to have a private conversation, and I'm eager to hear what he has to say.

He pats me on the shoulder. "Let's get you some fuel before we go."

Chapter Fifteen

JAMIE

I follow my uncle to the large wooden shelter in the center of camp. Built completely from naturally fallen trees provided by the forest, it serves as the pack's outdoor dining hall. There are several rows of long picnic tables and matching benches stretching from one end of the structure to the other. An area of water and other beverages sits at the back left corner, and to the right, there's a buffet style lineup of food.

I catch sight of Paloma's golden hair as she serves a line of elders. She spots me watching and gives me her signature sweet grin: closed lipped, cheeks full, and eyes closed. She always greets everyone with the same look, like a dog happy to see its owner after they've been gone for several hours.

Instead of walking over to say hi, Rhett leads me to an empty table away from all the others. A young girl with rich brown pigtails hurries over with a steaming cup of corn chowder and a stick of corn bread. "Paloma said this is for you," the girl tells me. She then skips away to join a small group of girls her age.

"This looks good," I say, mouth already salivating. "Has she made her award-winning white chicken chili yet?"

"Nah." Rhett scratches his beard thoughtfully. "Too early in the season."

I scoop a spoonful of chowder onto my spoon and swallow it. The delicious flavors of the base broth coat my tongue, and the sweet and soft texture of the corn mixed with lightly mashed potatoes slides down my throat with a warm comfort.

There are select werewolves in the pack who enjoy the thrill of a hunt in their wolf forms, but most try to satiate their hunger before each shift. I am one of the latter. I do not enjoy killing other creatures, even in a less human state of mind. Yet, when I think back to the moment Patrick was in my grasp, I was only a heartbeat away from ending his life, all for laying his hands on Raegan.

It would seem that she is unquestionably the defining factor when it comes to my rage. I wonder just how far I would be willing to go when it comes to protecting her. Would I attack my own pack? The question sends a shiver down my spine, and though I doubt they would ever do anything to hurt someone they knew was important to me, I pray I'm never in a situation that would force me to find out.

"So what did you want to talk to me about?" I ask in between mouthfuls of chowder. Rhett passes me a glass of water and I take giant gulps to wash down each bite. Then I grab the cornbread.

"What makes you think I want to talk?"

I give him an incredulous look. "You pulled me away from the others and gave me food so I would shut up and listen to whatever you have to say."

Rhett smirks and lifts his chin, proud to see I nailed his motives. Our relationship has always been like this. He tests me, and instead of giving him the answers he wants, I test him back.

His shoulders sag, making him appear smaller than the towering man I know. "I believe you are the one who has a question for me." His hands fold together on the table in front of him, weathered skin and broken nails on full display as he waits for me to ask the question he already knew was coming.

I clear my throat and wipe my mouth on the corner of my sleeve. "What were the signs when you found out Paloma was your mate?"

His eyes crinkle knowingly. "Is it Raegan?"

I'm momentarily caught off guard. "I was hoping *you* could tell me that."

A deep laugh escapes his chest and it forces me to relax. "Jamie, if you're asking me for what signs to look for, I'm pretty sure you already have an idea of who it is. Or better yet...who you want it to be."

This last part strikes me. "I have a choice?"

"In a way," Rhett alludes. "I believe we are presented with the mate our spirit believes would be the best match. But in the end, it is our hearts that decide. When the spirit finds a match, it reaches for its perfect companion like a separate hand reaching from your body. It can pull you in the direction it wants to go. But if you ignore that pull for too long, eventually your spirit will give up trying."

A pull.

It's the exact sensation I've been feeling toward Raegan. When I'm not by her side, it's as if my mind is trying to convince my body to go to her. But it's more than just my mind, or my heart, it's my spirit, my soul.

I must have an enamored expression on my face, because Rhett is now looking at me in absolute glee. I've never seen this man so goddamn happy before.

"So it is Raegan," he suggests coyly.

"What about her side in all this?" I ask. "Doesn't she get a say in whether or not she wants to be tied to me for the rest of her life?"

"That is where the choice comes into play," Rhett answers. "If your spirits truly are a match, they will both feel a pull toward one another. But it is possible for one spirit to feel a pull when the other does not."

Rhett glances at a man sitting at the end of a table to the right of us. He is surrounded by others talking animatedly about something they deem hilarious, but the guy doesn't seem too interested in the conversation. Every so often he'll nod along and fake a laugh, but the moment the others look away, his face falls back to a frown. He looks young, maybe in his early twenties, but something about him gives off a severe loneliness, and I want to know why.

Rhett soothes my curiosity, "Ezra thought he found his mate six months ago, but the bond was rejected. From what I know about the situation, he felt a love for Ezra, but I don't think he was ready for a lifelong commitment."

My heart sinks in my chest at the idea of Raegan having those same thoughts. We aren't as young as Ezra, but still...what if Raegan doesn't want to be tied to me in such a permanent way? We've never talked about how the other feels toward marriage and serious relationships. As just her friend, it's never been my place. But now...

"What if he changes his mind down the road? Could they still be mates?"

"I'm not sure," Rhett says curiously. "I've never seen it happen, but anything is possible, I suppose."

"You and Paloma were about their age when you mated. What made you feel ready?"

Rhett's face glows with the thought of his wife. I've never

seen a more true love between two people than the one I see with them. "I've never been one to question my gut," he says. "Back then, I had a gut feeling that I should never let her go, so I didn't."

"Seems simple enough," I mutter.

"The reason why I bring this up isn't to force you to make your decision. I just want you to be aware that having an unclaimed mate can create a vulnerability for us. The others might sense your desire to protect her as a challenge for dominance. I don't think many would try, but I know of one that might consider it."

As if he heard his name being called, Banks slowly cocks his head to stare at the back of Rhett's mane of red. Banks is one of the loudest who routinely labels me a rogue wolf. He's a mid-level delta, just like me, but if he could have his way, he'd challenge my status and call for my exile. He's always wanted to have more of a say in the pack. And if I'm not mistaken, I think he's had his eye on being beta for a while. Though as long as Rhett and Paloma are our leaders, I doubt they'll accept anyone but Woody by their sides. He may be an elder, but he's still our second strongest. No doubt Banks is just waiting for the day Woody passes.

"You think he would threaten Raegan?" I ask, referring to Banks.

"I think very few still consider you a member of this pack, and instead more like a loose string they want to cut."

The comment stings. I glance at Banks again, taking in his cocky smirk. He reminds me of Patrick, and immediately my blood starts to boil. "Why don't you put them in their place?" I growl. "They've seen my loyalty. I might not live with the pack, but I always come back."

"Packs are meant to be our family, Jamie, and family sticks together."

I scoff. "There are plenty of families who live apart," I say. "My mom and dad are in the city, but they're still my parents."

Before Rhett can give a retort, hurried footsteps race toward the shelter and skid to a halt just in front of where we're seated. A flushed teenage boy around the same age as Casey is breathing heavily and clutching his side.

"There's someone here to see you," the kid huffs, still trying to catch his breath.

I assume there's someone here for Rhett, but when I meet the young wolf's eyes, he's looking right at me.

Chapter Sixteen

RAEGAN

There's a tall and lanky nerd of a man wearing black framed glasses standing guard outside the entrance of the werewolf camp. I'm small, but I'm pretty sure if I really wanted to get by, I could knock this guy on his ass.

Currently, he's squinting at my face as if he's trying to place me.

"Need your prescription updated?" I ask, attempting humor.

The sound of my voice seems to trigger his memory, and finally the muscles in his scrunched expression soften to recognition. "Raegan! It's you!"

I tilt my head and further examine the man in front of me. If he knows me, shouldn't I know him? As I look him up and down, I take in his baggy jeans and ripped brown sweater. The yarn is fraying in multiple places, and there's a slit cut into the collar, whether on purpose or by accident, I'm unsure. His face does look familiar, and now I'm giving him the same scrutinizing expression.

I try to imagine him without the clothes. Not naked —*because eww*—but the style is throwing me off. Then it hits me.

"Tyler!" He beams once I've realized who is his. "Nerdy little Tyler Paulson. I used to babysit you when I was in high school!"

He blushes. "Still nerdy," he confesses shyly, pointing to his glasses. To me he's giving more of a scholarly skater style.

"You stopped my laptop from crashing when I had that major science paper due! Wow, you're all grown up." I take him in again. Puberty didn't necessarily fill him out, but it shot him to about six feet. "I heard you work at the tech store."

Tyler nods proudly. "Yep. I'm a Gadget Ghoul."

"I didn't know you were a werewolf."

For a second, I wonder if that was rude of me to say, but my attention is suddenly pulled to someone behind his right shoulder.

My stomach flutters.

A shirtless Jamie comes to stand behind Tyler and places a steady hand on his shoulder.

"Hey there, lemon," he greets me, voice rough with a longing I can't quite put my finger on, but the instant heat it elicits between my legs leaves no room for interpretation.

Holy shit. It's official: I want Jamie bad.

I've seen him without a shirt before, but not since my sexual enlightenment. Instead of just seeing him as a best friend who happens to be male, now I see him as...well, *very* male. I'm obsessed with the toned shape of his muscles and how they balance so well with his slender flame. He's not a buffed out body-builder, but the V cut beneath his abs is deliciously detailed.

Tyler steps away, a very different expression on his face

now that Jamie is here. He almost looks worried. He glances back at me and something clicks behind his eyes, then he scurries off into the camp.

What the hell just happened?

Jamie saunters over to where I'm standing at the edge of the property, but he does not look happy to see me. "What are you doing here?"

We both know my being here means I know things I shouldn't, but I don't know how to answer him.

"What made you..." He trails off, and I watch his eyes grow slowly in realization. "You feel it too, don't you?"

"Jamie," my voice wavers as I speak his name, "what's going on?"

He gives in and takes my hand, and I follow him through the camp past many wandering eyes. I think I hear a snarl or two, and Jamie quickens his step, forcing me to keep up at a brisk pace. His back muscles are clenched so tightly I can make out the entire structure of his shoulder blades. My being here is clearly making him upset, but it's too late for me to turn back now.

As we weave our way through mobile homes and tents, I find myself still trying to rationalize the situation. *Maybe he's friends with the werewolves, like he's friends with Aidan. Perhaps he comes here often.* Kendra mentioned his uncle is a werewolf, so maybe he just likes to visit his family.

Eventually, we reach a large wooden structure shaped like a bell tent at the far end of the camp, the top of which just barely sweeps the lowest branches of the surrounding trees. As we enter, I'm awestruck by the interior. There's a completely separate sleeping and kitchen area, along with a small table with four chairs.

Jamie gestures for me to take a seat at the table, so I do. He sits across from me, hands laced together on the table's surface with a pained expression on his face. His gaze falls to my own hands that are clasped in my lap, a little too properly, but I'm not sure what else to do with them. I've never once felt awkward around Jamie, but right now I feel as if my bones are trying to crawl out of my skin and run away.

"I think we both know why you're here," he starts, eyes still not looking away from my hands.

For some reason, his desire to jump right to the nitty gritty rubs me the wrong way. "You sound like you're about to give me detention."

I watch him fight the smallest smirk, but it's not enough to crack his serious expression.

Yes, I've most likely figured out why he's been keeping things from me and acting strangely all week long, but I don't want to skip over the fact that he did those things in the first place. He nearly ran out on me this morning, just after asking me to move in with him the day before. He might be ready to confess, but I'm not ready to gloss over the way he's made me feel.

"Why did you leave so quickly this morning?"

His eyes dart sideways, avoiding mine. "You know why," he states plainly.

I buckle down. "No I don't."

"You wouldn't be here if you didn't." With every word he says, his shoulders draw further and further in, like he's preparing for me to explode.

Maybe it's just because of spite, but I do just that. "Just say it, Jamie!"

My voice nears a shout, but I reel it back. I can feel myself slipping into an accusatory state, but I don't want Jamie to think I'm mad. I'm not mad. Maybe a little wounded that he didn't trust me, but not mad. I just want him to explain it to me. In his own words, not the ones I've come up with in my head.

"Please," I add quietly. My eyes linger on his bare chest again, and a need to touch him signals like a lighthouse in my mind. Not in a sexual way. I just want him to hold me. I need the reassurance of his warmth, of his strength.

He looks more pained now than when he first sat down. I can tell he doesn't like that he's made me upset. I watch as his hunched shoulders straighten, and his chest moves out and then slowly in as he takes a calming breath.

"You're right," he says quietly, finally meeting my eyes. "I'm sorry. I was hoping since you figured it out, we could skip this part." He smiles tentatively, turning into a wince. He closes his eyes. "But you deserve an explanation."

I force my gaze away from his chest and speak truthfully. "This has been one of the hardest, most confusing weeks of my life. I just need to know why."

He rubs his temples nervously. "I don't know why."

I frown and repeat his statement, trying hard to keep the bite out of my words. "You don't know."

"I mean, it's just..." He fumbles on his words. "I don't know why I hid it for so long. You've had a hard and confusing week because of me. I know that. But I can't give you a true reason behind it." His mouth twists into a sour expression. "I think there's always been a part of me that wishes I could hide from what I am. Not just from others, but from myself."

He uncrosses his arms from where they've been resting on the table and his hands lock into fists. I pull back slightly, but then he tucks them away beneath the table. Even when he's angry at himself, I know Jamie would never put me in harm's way.

"When we first met," I start, but then he answers by finishing my sentence for me.

"I didn't tell you because you seemed so against paranormals. The way you talked about your family—" I flinch, but he scoots his chair closer. "I'm not blaming you. I'm saying I took what you said as an excuse to continue to hide. I was still in denial at the time. We'd just moved to Shadow Hills. My entire life had been uprooted, and all because of something I couldn't control. So I didn't talk about it. I kept my wolf a secret, thinking that the more I pushed him down, eventually he'd just...go away. But he didn't."

"Your wolf." Saying it out loud feels almost freeing. Not quite there, but a positive step toward it.

He must see my need for confirmation in my face, because he nods carefully, then says, "Yes, Raegan. I'm a werewolf."

I thought the actual confession would elicit more of a reaction, but I feel nothing. I'm not even moved. I guess as I tried to process everything on the way here, in the back of my mind I already accepted what he is. And what he's always been, what he still is: my Jamie.

He drops his chin and pulls his arms back, tucking them close to his torso. "I'm afraid of losing control," he admits in a low tone. "It happens every month, and I'm afraid every time."

I lean in and lightly stoke his forearm. It hurts me to see him like this. So vulnerable. So fearful of himself. I can't imagine what that must feel like, having to relinquish control of your own mind and body. Not once, not twice, but every lunar cycle.

"Is that why you had a fever this morning?" I ask, still feeling the heat radiating off his skin. "Because your body is telling you it's time to shift?"

He nods. "I always end up fighting it until the last second."

He glances up, and when I follow his gaze I find a skylight in the center of the ceiling. Tonight, the view would be perfect for stargazing, but right now, it only serves as a reminder that

Jamie's time is almost up. The sun has spent most of the morning hiding behind rain clouds. The moon might not be visible, but it lingers out there on the horizon, inching closer and closer to its highest point in the sky.

Though I feel much better now that Jamie has actually spoken the words I needed to hear, my mind is still spinning with questions. And the next one comes out without thinking. "I don't understand how you've managed to hide this for so long. Who else knows?"

The tiniest smirk lifts the corner of his mouth. "The pack, obviously," he starts. "And Aidan."

"That's it?"

"Well, my parents. But yeah. That's it."

Suddenly I'm struck with a new fear and I can't help the panic in my voice. "Jamie, paranormals have to be registered. If the mayor doesn't know about you, you could get in serious trouble."

The words rush out of me frantically, as if Mayor Musthaven could burst through the wall at any moment. But Jamie takes my hand and gently starts rubbing circles into my palm.

"It's okay, Rae," he tells me. "I understand the risk."

"I thought you were going to start calling me lemon," I tease, my heart pumping loudly in my ears.

His lips part, and I follow the trail his tongue takes as it darts out to lick his bottom lip. "I'll save that for a different occasion."

My stomach does a somersault, and the new curious side of my brain wants to believe he's implying what my body hopes he's implying, but I can't be sure.

"So what happens now?" I ask, trying to ignore the sudden ache in my core.

Jamie swallows hard and gazes out the tent flap to the camp

beyond. "I have to shift. I can't wait it out much longer. But it's only for tonight. Then I'll be back to normal."

Back to normal.

I hate that he views this natural part of himself as *not* normal. Embracing what he is is one thing, but to embrace the act of losing himself over and over, that's another act of strength entirely.

Suddenly he winces as if he's gotten a sharp headache, and I notice he's sweating more profusely now. Rivulets of sweat run from his temple and down his toned chest.

"I know there's a lot you still want to know," he says, "but can we finish this conversation back at our place?" he asks, his tone extremely gentle, like he's holding a baby bird. "I promise I'll tell you everything. Right now, it's just getting harder for me to think straight."

It feels like years ago that Jamie asked me to move in and I officially accepted. But it was only yesterday.

"Of course." I stand up quickly and he rushes to my side.

"Go straight home, okay. It's not a good idea for you to linger."

His comment only makes me worry about him. What dangerous situation am I leaving him in?

"Is everything okay?"

He keeps his hand pressed to my lower back as he leads me through the camp, all the while keeping his eyes on those around us. "Yes, yes," he insists. "I'll be fine. It's you I'm worried about. I don't want you here when the others start to shift."

Suddenly I'm keenly aware that I'm in a literal den of wolves, and I'm reminded of what Aidan told me about werewolves losing their human morals after shifting. I walk a little faster as we near the front gate.

"You'll be there when I get back, right?" Jamie asks.

His sincerity is like a balm to my raw fear. *As if I'd be anywhere else.*

"Yes," I promise. "I will."

Chapter Seventeen

JAMIE

Knowing Raegan finally knows the truth has me in such a euphoric state, I almost forget about my need to shift. But the longer we sat across from one another in Rhett and Paloma's house, the tell-tale signs rushed to the forefront of my mind.

My temperature has probably skyrocketed just in the last five minutes, and now there's a sharp pounding against my temples making the sun too bright and any noise too loud.

Raegan promises she would wait for me at my condo—the one I can now call ours. This brings on another wave of relief, knowing she'll be safe while I let my wolf run free. The sudden onset migraine almost starts to feel like a mild pin prick at the thought of her being there when I get home. I'll finally be able to tell her everything I've had to keep hidden all these years, every internal struggle and difficult position I've been put in. Then maybe I can tell her about the bond.

I have no doubt that if she was able to figure out what I've been hiding, she's also figured out why I've been acting the way

I have. If she was compelled to find me, surely that means she feels the pull too. I want to ask her, but first, I have to get out of this scorching human body.

Rhett is waiting for us at the front entrance. Based on the shit-eating grin plastered across his face, he's probably deduced that the woman walking next to me is the mate I was questioning him about earlier.

"You must be Raegan," Rhett says, extending his hand to shake hers as we approach. "I'm Jamie's Uncle Rhett."

Her unblemished hand takes his weathered one and for a moment I think he might crush her delicate fingers. I can feel the growl climbing up my throat, but Rhett gives me a placating look, as if to say *chill out, I'm not hurting your girl.*

She's looking at me knowingly. "I didn't know you had family in Shadow Hills."

"Oh you know how the story goes," Rhett suggests. "Everyone's got that crazy uncle they don't like to talk about." He laughs heartily and Raegan doesn't bother fighting the smile that comes to her lips.

My nostrils flare, unamused. "Alright, that's enough. She was just leaving."

Raegan pulls back and crosses her arms in that tightly tucked protective shield she's so good at making. I've hurt her feelings by rushing her away, but she has to understand, I don't want her here when I lose control. I can't promise I won't accidentally hurt her somehow.

Compared to Rhett, I probably look like I've come down with a heinous flu. My uncle on the other hand is as calm and cool as a cucumber, with many decades of shifting under his belt. His control is much steadier than mine, and I envy his years of wisdom.

Rhett looks back and forth from Raegan's wounded expression to my clear desperation. I can't stop clenching and unclenching my hands, and though I shed my shirt, it feels like something is choking me, and I keep reaching to pull at an invisible collar.

Raegan's expression is now turning to concern. She takes a tentative step toward me, but I take an equal step back. And there's that hurt look again.

I finally get to tell her the truth, and now I'm fucking everything up.

"Okay, I think it's time we get this show on the road," Rhett says pointedly. He gently lays a hand on Raegan's shoulder and steers her toward the exit. "He'll be fine, darlin'," I hear him tell her as they get further away. "This isn't his first rodeo."

I let loose a sigh of relief and lift my eyes to the gray and gloomy sky. As the wind shifts the clouds, I catch the faint outline of my nemesis, and my stomach lurches.

Glancing around frantically, I check to see if anyone else is around, but the camp has scattered. No friends eating and chatting happily at picnic tables. No kids running wildly through trees disobeying their parents. The camp is a ghost town, except for me and the blurred outline of my uncle coming back into view. Without me realizing, my vision has started to glaze over. Everything is out of focus, even as I raise my hand right in front of my face I can barely make out the lines along my palm.

I've never waited this long to shift before. Typically, if I put it off until the day of, I'm already running through the trees first thing that morning, but it's almost noon and I can feel my wolf clawing beneath my skin, begging for freedom.

As Rhett reaches my side, he firmly grips my bicep, and I can hear the animalistic shift in voice as he says, "Now, boy."

At those words, my wolf lifts its head and howls. I hear him calling out to the moon, but then I realize the high-pitched yell is coming from me. The line of where I end and the wolf begins has already blurred beyond recognition, and the last thing I see as my body and mind succumb to the beast is the tunnel of trees around me as I dart on all fours into the woods.

Chapter Eighteen

RAEGAN

As I'm walking back to my car, I hear the distinct sound of a wolf howling from within the camp. My first instinct is to run, but knowing that howl might be coming from Jamie sends my heart racing. The rational side of my brain is telling me to leave him be—Rhett was right, this isn't the first time he's shifted, so Jamie knows what he's doing—but the irrational side wants to run straight into his arms.

He's not in any danger, I try to tell myself.

But if that's the case, why does it feel like my heart is trying to burst from my chest? It's pounding with panic against my rib cage, and with every pump of muscle rushing blood to my ears, all I hear is, *help him, help him.* It follows my heart's rhythm, and every second I ignore it, the warning only pumps harder.

We didn't have much time to truly talk about everything, but from what little he described, it sounded as if he's living his worst nightmare every month. Losing control of his mind must be terrifying, and it's happening to him right now.

What if he needs me?

Perhaps if I just gave him the opportunity to see me,

without getting too close, it would help calm him somehow. If I keep my distance, I'll be okay.

Just a glimpse, and then I'll go.

Any self-preservation skills I learned growing up fly out the window as I race back to camp just as the clouds above me break and rain starts to fall. As I pass the entrance, suddenly I realize I'm not just dealing with one werewolf. If I go any further, I could be facing an entire pack.

I feel the hairs on the back of my neck lift in alert as I skid to a halt. What once was spotty sprinkles falling from the sky is now turning into a steady drizzle. I search wildly around me for any hint of danger, but all is quiet save for the faint plops of water falling onto roofs. Then I hear the subtle shifting of gravel behind me. Keeping my back to whoever, or whatever, lingers behind me, I slowly turn my head to look over my shoulder.

Chin lowered and tail sticking straight back, a sandy colored wolf more than half my size is crouched behind me. Its legs are notched at the joints, its posture leaning forward slightly as if it's getting ready to pounce, and I immediately stiffen.

Slowly, I turn my body fully to face the predator before me. It's when I see the color of its eyes that I let out a gasp.

Warm brown, like thick honey.

"Jamie?"

The wolf cocks its head and snarls, teeth bared, and my stomach tightens nervously, but I hold my ground. I watch as it takes me in. I can't be sure, but I think I see its eyes soften just slightly. Its tail lowers a few inches and it begins to pace back and forth in front of me, so I remain perfectly still, not wanting to scare it or trigger any reason to attack.

But then those honey-colored eyes meet mine, and every

muscle in my body relaxes at once. I no longer feel frightened of the monster in front of me. I feel safe.

My right hand lifts of its own accord and reaches out, palm up, as an offering—a plea to let the creature know it too is safe with me. I feel myself kneeling to the earth, and an eternity moves around us as we stare into what feels like each other's souls. I don't know how to explain it, but I *know* Jamie is in there. No matter how deep, I can feel him reaching out for me. So when the wolf moves his two front paws and carefully steps into my reach, I hold my breath.

The dense fur on his muzzle grazes my palm, his breath hot against my skin. I'm shaking uncontrollably now, unable to contain my nerves. But he doesn't hurt me. Instead, he presses his snout further into my hand and rubs his head against my inner arm.

"It is you, isn't it?"

The wolf—Jamie—responds with a measured whine, and I let out a disbelieving chuckle. My head lowers when I feel tears of happiness brimming in my eyes, but Jamie moves to comfort me by resting the full weight of his head on my shoulder. I instinctively wrap my arms around his warm body and breathe in the scent of musk and freshly fallen rain. It's coming down harder now, causing thick strands of my hair to stick to my face. I'm shivering from the cold and on the brink of majorly freaking out, yet I've never felt more at ease.

Suddenly, Jamie barks loudly and I have to pull back to cover my ear. "What'd you do that for?"

But he isn't looking at me. His steady gaze is focused solely on the trees behind me. I turn to search for whatever has him concerned, but I can't see anything beyond the haze of mist along the treeline. A deep vibration rises from the back of his throat—a warning growl to stay away. I wipe rain from my face as it starts to come down in sheets, and for a split second, I see the outline of several other wolves prowling the far end of camp. Jamie's pack has come to get him, it's time for me to go.

Jamie moves in front of me, attempting to block me from their view, but a dark gray wolf steps out from the fog. From where I'm standing, this wolf looks slightly larger than Jamie. Both predators have their canines bared in warning, but the gray wolf almost looks like it's smirking.

The gray wolf takes a taunting step forward, and Jamie lets out a short, guttural bark. I don't know who the pack member is, but Jamie is not happy about them being here.

"It's okay," I tell him, placing a hand tentatively on his back. He cranes his neck to look at me from the corner of his eye, still keeping his body facing the threat ahead of him. "Go with them."

The gray wolf finally turns away, knowing Jamie won't leave my side. Jamie sits back on his hind legs as I get to my feet. He whimpers and paws at my leg, leaving a smear of dirt on my jeans.

"I'll be waiting for you," I say.

I watch as he gives me one last look, and then bounds off to catch up with the rest of the pack. As I watch him leave, a laugh bubbles out of me. I've lived among werewolves my whole life, but this is the first time I've ever seen one in their wolf form. They're so majestic and powerful, seeing them up close only makes me want to learn more about them. I can't wait to pick Jamie's brain about everything when he gets back.

I feel a lump form in my throat at the thought of being separated from him until tomorrow, but I no longer have any doubt that he'll come home the first moment he's able. When he does, I'll be waiting.

Chapter Nineteen

JAMIE

My joints ache as I take the four steps up to my front door the next morning. I can still feel the chill in my bones from running through the damp, cold forest all night. Though my body is perfectly capable of handling such conditions as a wolf, my fragile human form is not. It's as if I've run a marathon in a monsoon, and now I'm paying the price.

I take a seat on the top step and lean back against the railing to try and catch my breath, but my sinuses are completely blocked. I have to breathe through my mouth to fill my lungs, and my sense of smell is shot. My hearing must still be in working order though, because when I discern the subtle click of the door unlocking, I jump to my feet.

Raegan appears behind the storm door clad in an old T-shirt I grabbed from a volunteer job one summer. It's a heather gray color with SHADOW HILLS written in block letters across the front. It falls past her hips and covers the top half of her worn leggings. It's 6:30 in the morning, and her eyes appear bloodshot with deep circles beneath. I hope she didn't stay up all night waiting for me.

But as soon as I see her familiar smile, I lose any care in the world. Right now, I just want to get past the door that's blocking me from her warm embrace.

She must have the same inclination, because as soon as she unlocks the latch and turns the handle, she's jumping into my arms. I'm overwhelmed with the smell of coconut in her hair and the sweet, vanilla-like scent of her bare skin. It's not lotion or perfume, just her natural smell, and it makes me think she'd taste just as sweet if I ever got the chance to find out.

As I bury my face into her neck, I have to fight the urge to taste her right here, but we aren't there yet. Though we've taken a step toward the place we both know we're headed, it doesn't mean she's ready to start running. I know Raegan feels the same pull that I do, but I doubt she fully understands. Though it feels like I've been waiting for years, I have to take my time with her.

If I mess this up, our friendship will never recover.

Raegan pulls back to look me in the face as she runs her hands over my damp clothes. Her touch triggers a shiver to race down my spine, but I pointedly ignore it.

"You're soaked," she says. She ushers me across the threshold, into the house, and all the way up the stairs to my en suite bathroom. "Go ahead and take a warm shower, and I'll make you some coffee."

I ignore her instructions and pull her into the bathroom with me. "Did you stay up all night?"

She answers quietly. "No, but I didn't sleep well. I woke up around five and decided to just wait for you downstairs."

I cup her cheek in my hand. "Why didn't you sleep well? You weren't worried about me, were you?" I tease.

She nods shyly, embarrassed that I've called her out. I was only kidding, but I guess I hit a little too close to home.

"Rae." I take my other hand and hold both sides of her face, playfully shaking her head to the beat of my words. "You. Don't. Need. To. Do. That."

She steps out of my grip and I worry I've made fun of her concern when it's genuine.

"This whole wolf life might not be new to you, but it is to me," she says, crossing her arms protectively against her chest. "I don't know what warrants worry and what doesn't. So, if you're really going to tell me everything, it needs to start with that."

She's right. I feel like shit for not taking into consideration how this might affect her anxiety. She probably slept terribly because she was lying in bed thinking about all the things that might be happening to me out there in the woods, things she's never had to consider before. After being unable to leave her house for two days because of Patrick, why on earth did I expect her to take this news so easily?

Jamie, you're such a fucking idiot.

"I'm so sorry, Rae. Really." I pull her into another hug. "My mind and body go haywire if I don't shift when I'm supposed to, so it's difficult to think about anything else. I wanted to explain everything to you yesterday, but there just wasn't time."

"I know that now," she mumbles against my chest. "I just wish I could have put it all together sooner. I had no time to process. Once I realized what you are, you were already changing in front of me." She pauses thoughtfully, but peers up at me with those beautiful blue eyes of hers. "I wanted to talk to my best friend about all this, but the wolf took you away."

That punches me in the gut.

"Hey. I am *always* your best friend. Even if you can't see

me, I'm still in there. Sometimes I have to let the wolf take the wheel, but that doesn't mean I'm not in the car."

She rolls her eyes and steps out of my arms. "Nice analogy."

I shrug. "I thought it made sense."

"Did you—" She fumbles for her next words. "Do you remember anything when you're in that form?"

"You mean once I come back? Yeah. But it's different. It doesn't play out in my head like it does when I'm human. My memories as a wolf rely on the five senses, and feelings. I remember what I was feeling more than anything."

"And what did you feel this time?"

It looks like she's waiting for me to say something specific, but I just say the first thing that comes to mind.

"Peace," I tell her, voice quiet. "I normally resent my time as a wolf, because of how much control I have to relinquish, but this time I just felt peace." I swallow the lump in my throat. As I try to focus back on the past twenty-four hours, something else comes to me. A smell. *Her* smell. "You were there, weren't you? You didn't leave."

She scratches her neck nervously and averts her gaze. "I stayed long enough to watch you turn. But you saw me, and you—"

Panic seizes me. "Did I hurt you?"

"No."

Her answer is quick, so I release the breath I'm holding.

Then she adds, "You recognized me. You made me feel safe."

The relief that washes over me feels like a thousand pounds falling from my shoulders. Our bond must be a lot stronger than I thought. One of my biggest fears when shifting is what I might do to those around me, yet my selfish desire to push it off until the last minute only puts those I love in more danger.

"I'm glad you felt that way with me, but that doesn't mean you're safe around the others. I don't want you going back to the camp."

Her eyes narrow in scrutiny.

I never want to be the type of man to tell a woman what to do, but this is important, and I need her to understand. Yet right now, I can hardly hold my eyes open.

"I'm sorry. I'll explain everything, just—" I give myself a once over, "can I take a shower first?"

Her face softens and she grabs a towel out from the small closet beside her. She knows this house like she knows her own, and now it's hers too.

"Just sit right there," I say, pointing to the edge of the tub. "I'll be five minutes."

My en suite bathroom is slightly smaller than the guest bath, but it came with a miniature clawfoot tub customized to fit the space. I heard the previous owner's wife had severe arthritis and needed the tub to soak her aching joints, but I've yet to use the thing. Now I can't stop myself from visualizing sharing it with Raegan.

Raegan's cheeks go pink, and I can sense she's about to protest, but I stop her by saying, "Just close your eyes if you don't want to look." Though by the subtle shift in her scent, I think she does.

I immediately start stripping away my damp and reeking clothes, not waiting to see if she's going to stay, but once I climb into the shower and close the curtain, I take a quick peek to see her sitting stiffly on the edge of the tub.

My shower curtain is mostly opaque, but the top third is somewhat see-through, like looking through fogged glass. I can make out the outline of Raegan's form outside the shower, but I can't see the details of her face. Just the thought of her being only a few feet away while I'm buckass naked has my dick swelling.

"You alright there, lemon?" I ask, making sure she's not overthinking the hell out of this. It might seem like I'm being lewd, but I only want to keep her close while still respecting her boundaries.

"Back to that are we?" she says in a flat tone.

I smirk to myself, knowing she secretly loves that I've started calling her that. "Just testing the waters."

A beat passes before she speaks again. "It's awfully steamy."

My breath catches. "What?"

"The water. You've got the temperature up pretty high."

I hadn't noticed—my own temperature is only just now leveling back out to normal range—but she's right. The mirror is definitely covered with moisture and the air feels thick. "My bad." I adjust the faucet to keep from chasing her out with all the steam.

Several more minutes pass in silence.

"Your soap smells nice," she says quietly. I don't respond because I'm currently drowning my face under the spray of water. "Very manly."

I almost choke on the water as I laugh out loud. I can't stop the cough that invades my chest, and suddenly the shower curtain is ripped open to reveal a severely concerned looking Raegan.

"Are you alright?" she asks desperately. She hasn't quite registered that I'm completely naked, given that she apparently thought I was dying.

I lean forward and pound my fist against my chest to clear my throat. "I'm fine," I insist between gasps of air. "Just swallowed some water."

When I stand up straight, she's no longer looking at my

face. Her eyes are trained south, right where my semi is on full display. She hurriedly looks away, face blotchy either from the steam or embarrassment. I would bet a million dollars it's the latter.

"Sorry. I just...I thought something was wrong."

"Nothing wrong with taking a peek, lemon. It's yours whenever you want it to be." I can't believe how forward I'm being, but now that she knows about me being a werewolf, it's as if the door between us is wide open. For so long it was slightly cracked, allowing me to have wandering thoughts about what *could be* while we remained just friends. But now, what's stopping me from crossing that threshold?

Her, you idiot. It needs to be her decision.

She lets go of the curtain, letting it fall back into place without saying a word. "I'll let you finish up. I'm going to go make us some breakfast."

"Raegan, wait!" But it's too late. I hear the soft click of the bathroom door and know she's already gone.

I glance down at my dick, now losing its nerve. "Down boy."

I'm seriously going to have to learn some restraint.

Chapter Twenty

RAEGAN

I thought I could handle the amount of change that has been happening between us, but maybe I was wrong. Seeing Jamie naked and...excited—for *me*—it's just all too much.

Only a few days ago, we were still the same Raegan and Jamie we've always been. Now, not only do I have to adjust to the fact that he's somehow been a werewolf this entire time without telling me, but at some point I need to acknowledge this romantic pull that's formed between us.

I'm able to distract my sinful thoughts momentarily while I whip up some cheesy scrambled eggs and avocado toast, a simple breakfast I know Jamie likes. By the time I'm placing it all on a plate, he appears in the kitchen wearing a plain black T-shirt and gray sweatpants.

Great. That outfit will definitely help calm my runaway libido.

His eyes are heavy now, and I can tell the shower has relaxed him. He's no doubt ready for a long nap after an even longer night. I hate to be selfish and keep him up, but I can't wait another minute without getting the answers I need.

I place the plate down on the table in front of him and he sits, muttering a quick "Thank you" before digging into the eggs with his fingers. I poke his shoulder with the dull end of the fork in my hand and he takes it with a sheepish grin, mouth full.

I choose the seat next to him and wait patiently as he stuffs himself. It doesn't take long. As he's swallowing his last bite, I get up to pour him a cup of water and hand it to him. He downs it just as quickly.

Another quiet moment passes, then he looks at me with an open, inviting gaze. "Well, what do you want to know first?" he asks.

I try to think of the most pressing questions that have come to mind since yesterday. I'm curious about a lot of things, but I guess I should be most concerned with the parts that affect me.

"So," I start, "you turn every month." It's not a question, I just need his confirmation.

"Every full moon, yes."

"And how long do you spend in your," I gesture my hand wildly trying to come up with the appropriate words, "other body?"

Jamie's eyes crinkle at my gesturing. "It's up to me. Technically, I can shift whenever I want, but I choose not to. It's only during the peak of the moon's cycle that I have no other choice."

"So the moon *makes* you change?"

"The closer it gets to being completely full, the harder it is for me to resist shifting. I try to wait as long as I can, but," his head dips, "it was harder this time."

"Because of me?" I don't know why I've come to that

conclusion, but it just makes sense. Maybe Aidan is right. Maybe Jamie and I are mates.

After all, this new feeling between us has to mean *something*.

Jamie looks at me inquisitively, searching for something I have a feeling he already knows is there. "Do you mind if I ask *you* something?"

I shake my head and wait.

"Have you felt differently toward me this week? Feelings you've never felt before. Maybe a desire to be close to me."

This time I nod, achingly slow.

"What does it feel like: the feeling? Can you describe it?"

I already know the word, so I don't have to think too hard. "It's a pull," I tell him. "I feel like when we aren't together, I'm still being pulled toward you."

He looks to the ceiling and rubs his chin thoughtfully. Then his head drops and he stares at his own hands, as if they've done something without his permission. "It started after Patrick, right?"

I don't have to answer, because he already knows it's true.

"Raegan, there are some things about being a werewolf that are hard to explain to those who've never experienced it."

I know what he's getting at, so I decide to drop the most important question right on the table where we both will have to face it. "Am I your mate?"

He sucks in a breath and grabs the tops of his thighs aggressively, then he breathes out, and all that tension melts away. "I'm thinking that's a pretty good possibility."

It's such a massive realization, yet his confirmation is so blunt. Perhaps he's already accepted our circumstances, while I am only just now beginning to process it.

"Okay," I draw out slowly. "What does that mean exactly?"

Jamie takes his time formulating an explanation, but I can tell there are depths to this that even he can't quite explain.

"Simply put," he says, "we're bonded. Fated to be together." He turns in his seat to face me full on. "But that isn't a prison sentence, Rae. We're not stuck together. We both have a choice in this. It's just..." His voice trails off as his eyes land on my mouth. I'm nervously biting my lip, and it seems to have distracted him. "Werewolves live in pairs," he continues after refocusing. "It's just how it is. We all, at some point, have an obligation to find our partner, but they don't have to be the one our souls are pulled to."

Again, he mentions *the pull*. Only, this time, it's in relation to the soul. Is it truly my soul that's trying to tell me to be with Jamie? If so, this bond he speaks of feels more metaphysical than just an act of nature.

I swallow the lump that's formed in my throat as I play with the edge of my T-shirt. Jamie's T-shirt. When I got back to Jamie's condo, I took a shower and changed into dry clothes. I found a worn but comfy pair of leggings left in my drawer to wear, but I didn't have a clean shirt, so I borrowed one of Jamie's tees from his closet. His lingering scent is all over the material—the same woodsy musk I smelled before, only now it's mixed with the undertones of powdery soft detergent. It brings me back to the feel of that same smell wrapped around me as I slept in his bed, waiting for him to come home.

The words he's saying make perfect sense, but my senses are so muddled by his presence, I can hardly bring myself to focus on them.

"So our souls are meant to be together," I suggest, then add, a bit quieter, "romantically."

He nods.

"But we don't have to be together, physically, if we don't want to."

He nods again. "Right."

I wish there were a better way of going about this. A class we could take in which we are provided a complete list of instructions on how to act and what to say, now that we are no longer considered to be just friends. Though we haven't acted on it, the desire is clearly there. I feel it like sticky sweat clinging to the back of my neck brought on by Jamie's eyes as they radiate his clear desire to undress me.

He might be fully clothed now, but the image of him in the shower is plastered to my subconscious like a poster of my favorite boy band in my childhood bedroom.

His eyes turn downward, probably to keep himself from continuing to stare. "We're compatible. Why wouldn't we be?" Then I see his eyelids flutter upward, and he's focused back on me. "You're my best friend. I can't think of anyone else I'd rather be mated with than you."

While his sentiment is well-intended, instead of thinking about how well suited we are as a pair because of our emotional connection, my brain goes straight to how compatible we'd be in bed.

Suddenly my cheeks are burning. My epidermis is sending out an emergency flare in the form of flushed skin, basically saying *'Help! She's overheating from arousal!'*

I stand up quickly and take Jamie's empty plate to the sink to rinse off. I can feel his eyes on my back, and now I'm very keenly aware that I'm not wearing a bra. When I turn back around, Jamie will most definitely spot the peaks of my hardened nipples through his T-shirt.

"This is what I was afraid of," he murmurs quietly.

Whether it was his intention for me to hear or not, I don't know, but now he's getting up from the table. I hear his steps shuffle closer, and then he's close enough that I can feel his breath on my neck.

"I never wanted any of this to freak you out," he says.

My shirt is clinging to my back from sweat. Now I feel like I'm the one running a temperature.

"This pull we both feel toward one another," he starts, "we can ignore it. We can move on like none of this ever happened." Gently, I feel his fingers trail the edge of my hip as I face the sink. "If that's what you want to do, I promise I will respect your wishes." His voice turns huskier. "But my wolf likes you. He wants to be near you." Then I feel his lips brush the shell of my ear as he whispers, "And so do I."

My grip slackens around the plate I'm holding and it clatters noisily into the sink. I don't care that there are more important conversations that need to be had, and I certainly don't care whether or not the stars are trying to dictate who I'm meant to be with. Right now, the only thing that matters is the infinitesimal amount of space between us as Jamie inches closer.

I need to know what his lips feel like.

I need to know what his body feels like pressed against mine.

He takes a handful of my hair and pulls it away from my neck, then gently, *painfully*, he places a single kiss to my clammy skin.

The sigh that comes from me is enough to assure him I'm okay with what he's doing, because he finally closes the gap and presses himself against me, flattening us against the edge of the counter.

He groans deeply against the back of my neck. "The moon has been driving me crazy, but I haven't been able to stop thinking about what it would be like to fuck you, Raegan."

Wetness pools between my legs. His voice alone is enough to make me slick with want. It's such an anomaly, hearing those words come from the mouth of someone I've known as only a friend for so long. It's taboo and hushed like a forbidden thing that should never be spoken aloud, and yet he does with such confidence.

I want to hear more of it. I want to break every rule that's ever been set between two friends since the dawn of time, because if I spend one more second like this with Jamie's growing erection pressed against my ass, I might combust. We could create our own galaxy with the amount of tension that's boiling between us. Another big bang. More moons than either of us can count.

"Do you think about it?" he asks, voice husky and low. It grates against my skin like sandpaper, raising all the hairs along my neck. He moves, and then I again feel his lips along the shell of my ear. "Please tell me you do."

I should be on the edge of another anxiety attack right now. This is all too different, too uncharted. Instead, I'm on the edge of his words as if they're a cliff, and I'm ready to jump off.

"Yes."

My voice is all but a whisper. I don't even know if he's heard me, but then his head dips and he's pressing his forehead into the back of my shoulder. He lets out another pained groan. He's questioning this just as much as I am, but if he doesn't make a move in the next five seconds, I might just have to do it for him.

"This is crazy. How did we get here, Rae?"

I shake my head and grip the edge of the sink tightly to keep my hands from shaking, the urge to grab him so strong, this magnetic pull that just keeps getting stronger. "I don't know," I say, "but I don't want to go back."

Finally, I've spoken the magic words. Jamie spins me around to face him and cups my cheek with one hand, the other still latched to my hip. "You want this?" he asks, needing my spoken consent. "You're absolutely sure?" I nod, my arms reaching instinctively for him, but it's not enough. "I need to hear you say it, Raegan."

This is it. It's time to jump. I swallow hard, focusing on the softness of his lips and the sweat beading on his brow. "Yes. I want this." Then add in an embarrassing whimper. "Please."

Jamie unleashes himself upon me, like a wolf freed from a cage. His mouth collides with mine, and all the breath rushes from my lungs. He tastes sweet and feral. Every slide of his lips along mine sends a rush of longing to my core. As he kisses me, his hands slip to my thighs and lift me up. I wrap my legs around his waist for leverage as he places me gently on the counter.

"Fuck," he growls, moving his lips to my jaw and beneath my chin. "I need to touch you. Can I take these off?" He's tugging at my leggings, so I lift my hips and allow him to pull them down my legs. They get caught on my ankles and I giggle as he dramatically yanks them free and tosses them onto the kitchen table, knocking over a salt shaker in the process.

"That's bad luck," I say before sliding my fingers through the soft strands of his hair.

His head tips back and his eyes close at the feel of my nails scratching against his scalp. "I'll burn some incense."

"I can get you a discount at my cousin's shop."

"Such generosity," he teases with a grin. "How can I repay you?"

His hands roam from my hips to my inner thighs, slowly spreading them further apart. The moment he touches the fabric of my underwear he'll be able to feel how wet I am. My first instinct is to be embarrassed, but then the feeling flits away like a hummingbird on a breeze. This is easy. This isn't a hookup with a stranger, this is Jamie. I can be honest, and right now I want him to know what his actions are doing to me.

My gaze drops to where his fingers are poised along the

lining of the fabric that's still hiding what he wants to feel. He said he needed to touch me. All he has to do is move half an inch.

Jamie follows my line of sight, and together we watch as his thumb slowly dips beneath the front of my underwear and slides between my seam. My gasp is far too loud, but I can't look away. I'm slick with want. His thumb easily glides along the inside of my lips until he reaches my clit, and then he presses down. Pleasure floods my core and more wetness pools beneath his touch.

"You're so eager for me," he murmurs. "I'm not even inside you yet."

He continues to slide his thumb along the same path he traced, adding gentle pressure each time he comes in contact with my clit. I want to keep watching the movements, but my eyes flutter closed, and it's getting harder to hold my head up. I lean back and rest my head against the cabinet door, then Jamie surprises me by slipping his thumb inside me.

Before my moan has a chance to subside he's already pulled back out. "You feel too good. I need to see what I do to you, not just feel it." Then he grips the waistband of my underwear and removes them completely.

Now that I'm bare before him, he takes no time plunging two fingers inside me. My mouth opens to let out a gasp but no sound comes out. I'm overstimulated, gasping for air. He pulls his fingers out slowly, coated in my glistening arousal, then dips them back in, each time stroking my inner walls in search of the perfect spot. Meanwhile, his opposite hand retains its place-ment on my outer thigh, holding me in place. The pressure is building in my core, and the muscles in my stomach start to clench. I need the soothing comfort of his lips while his fingers achingly guide me up to the peak of my climax.

I'm panting desperately. "Kiss me?"

His eyes meet mine with tenderness. "You never have to ask."

So I lean in and melt into his kiss. His tongue sweeps into my mouth searching, exploring with languid strokes. But I still need more. I'm teetering on the precipice, but something is keeping me from falling.

"Harder."

Jamie fingers slam into me with his next thrust and I actually let out a pornographic moan. It's instinctual. He pounds forcefully against my core, intentionally pressing hard against my clit as he moves, and soon my inner walls are screaming. A flutter builds and builds and then it takes flight. I'm coming harder than I ever have with the tools at my own disposal, and I cry out from the intensity of it, my arms on Jamie pulling him into me, panting into his shoulder.

He continues plunging into me, pulling away from me to take my jaw in his other hand to hold me steady enough to continue our kiss. Our mouths are open, sloppily sharing air and spit and I can't get enough of it. He presses himself against the inside of my thigh, and I feel his erection begging for friction. Finally, he heaves me over the peak and continues stroking me through the full wave of my orgasm before pulling away.

Jamie takes a step back, disconnecting from me for the first time since the initial kiss. His face is flushed and we're both panting from the intensity of what just happened.

"That was–"

"So fucking good," he finishes for me.

Speaking for myself, I wholeheartedly agree. Even though I'm spent, muscles loose like jelly, my next thought is to take care of him. But when I glance down at where his erection was just clearly outlined in his sweatpants, now there's a dark spot of wetness.

"Y-you came?" I stutter. "But how?"

He moves back to stand between my legs. I'm still spread openly on the counter like a buffet, but the look on his face is no longer consumed with desire. My best friend is looking at me, and I feel safe.

"You, Raegan," he says. "Just you."

Chapter Twenty-One

JAMIE

Well *shit.*

Now that I've had a taste of what Raegan looks like completely undone, I can never go back. Tiny strands of dark hair are plastered to her temple and her skin is flushed from cheeks to chest. She looks sexy as hell.

Raegan shifts uncomfortably on the counter, and I can tell she's ready to get down, so I take her by the waist and lower her carefully to the floor. Seeing her stand in my kitchen in just my shirt, the insides of her thighs caked in the arousal I caused, sends a rev to my dick to start up again, but I can't push it. All of this, no matter what I feel, has to be on her terms.

She wipes the stray hairs from her face and looks as exhausted as I feel. It's then that I remember I've been awake for more than twenty-four hours.

I see that the clock now reads 7:15 A.M. "Take a nap with me?" I suggest.

She nods and I lead her back upstairs to my bedroom. I grab a damp washcloth, knowing she'll want to clean up a bit, and wipe down her thighs before tucking her under the covers.

"Don't look so proud of yourself," she chastises playfully.

I must be smiling.

"How can I not be? I know what you smell like when you're turned on." I press one kiss to her lips and playfully bite her bottom lip. "Now I can't wait to taste you."

I change into a clean pair of briefs before climbing beneath the silky sheets beside her. I'm overwhelmed with her scent, but it must just be because she's here with me.

Next to me, Raegan's body is stiff, unsure whether or not she should keep space between us, so I reach out sleepily and grab her waist. "Come here."

She gives in and melts into my side. Pulling her back flush against my chest, I rest my chin on the top of her shoulder and breathe in the sweet scent of her coconut shampoo. I envision doing the same in my wolf form, and whether I'm dreaming or reliving a memory, I can't be sure. But the position soothes me, and soon I'm drifting back into a peaceful sleep, my best friend in my arms.

THE NEXT TIME I open my eyes, the clock reads 7:00 A.M. I shoot up in bed, confused and unsure whether I've gone back in time or the clock has stopped working. Turns out it's neither, because when I grab my phone the lock screen shows the date on the calendar has changed. I slept an entire day and night.

But where is Raegan?

Did she wake up early this morning and regret what we did yesterday?

I bring up her contact info to call her, and I see she's already sent me a text message. Several in fact.

THURSDAY 12:04 P.M. Hey you were still sound asleep so I just wanted you to know I'm back at my place to start packing 😺

THURSDAY 12:12 P.M. I am still moving in right?? Does our encounter on the counter mean we shouldn't? Ha

THURSDAY 12:13 P.M. ok that was a joke but seriously. Should we talk about this first?

THURSDAY 12:44 P.M. I know you're probably still sleeping so I'm just going to wait and we'll talk about it this evening 🩶

MISSED CALL 7:10 P.M.

THURSDAY 7:35 P.M. Hey so I came to check on you and you're still asleep. I don't know how long werewolves are supposed to rest after shifting, but you definitely didn't mention anything about hibernation.

THURSDAY 9:00 P.M. Can you call me when you get up so I know you're alive???

THURSDAY 11:20 P.M. I got a hold of Rhett and asked him if this was normal and apparently it is. I will come by in the morning.

THURSDAY 11:22 P.M. goodnight 🩶

The second I finish reading, I dial her number.

She answers on the second ring. "Jamie?"

"Who else would it be?" I tease, my voice scratchy.

She lets out a massive sigh on the other end of the line, her breath creating a loud crackling sound through the speaker. "I wish I would have known you were going to sleep for twenty-four years."

"Just twenty-four hours, Rae," I tease her, then I think

better of it. I know she probably tossed and turned half the night worrying about me. "Sorry, I should have warned you."

"It's okay," she says quietly. "How are you feeling?"

It's a loaded question. If she's asking about how my body is recovering from the shift, I feel fully rested and almost back to normal. But if she's asking about us—what we did—I'm worried I might say the wrong thing. Part of me is still afraid I'll spook her and send her running, but ultimately, I know I need to be honest. So, I tell her the truth.

"I'm good, Rae. What about you?"

"Me too."

I can hear the grin in her tone, and I just know she's probably smiling to herself like a giddy school girl with a crush. I love the idea of giving her butterflies, like we just met and are slowly learning things about each other one day at a time. In a way, I guess that's true. From here on out, I will be learning and exploring a new side of Raegan that I've never had permission to see before.

As long as she lets me.

"I'm glad to hear it," I tell her, as I get up from the bed. "I guess that means you can start packing again."

A beat passes, and I swear I feel a batch of butterflies in my own stomach.

Then she agrees. "I guess it does."

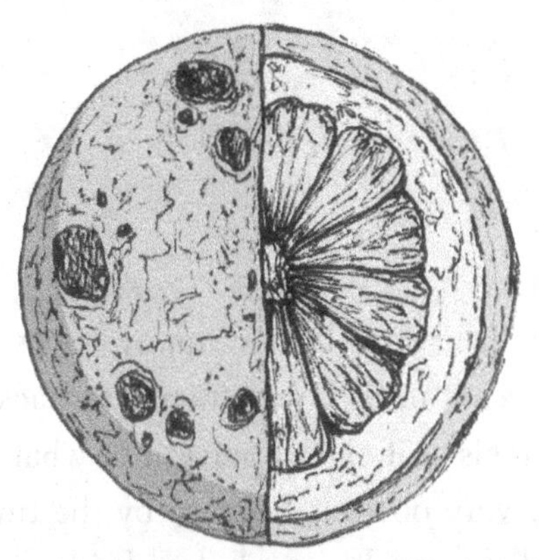

PART THREE:
Waning

Chapter Twenty-Two

RAEGAN

I hadn't realized exactly how many books I accumulated over the years until I was forced to pack them all into boxes. It feels as if eighty percent of what I own is books. This was made very obvious because by the time Jamie and I finish hauling them into his condo late Friday afternoon, there are only three boxes of household items and a suitcase left.

"Where are your clothes, Rae?" he asks, clearly out of breath.

I feel bad for making him carry my heavy boxes up and down the stairs, but I can't deny how good his arms look under the weight. I keep finding new parts of Jamie that send an ache through my core. Like the veins in his hands and forearms.

As my eyes train on the tight grip he has on the box he's carrying, I'm instantly transported back to when those same hands were gripping my thighs, and I can't believe I spent over fifteen years ignoring all the gloriously attractive parts of him.

I refocus my lustful thoughts to his lingering question. "That's what the suitcase is for," I tell him, tossing my thumb over my shoulder.

It's sad but true.

My closet leaves little to be desired. It certainly wouldn't grab the attention of any influencers. The last time I cared about what I wore was in middle school. I had a uniform all through high school and then immediately started working. Other than the flowy tops and jeans I wear at Bound and Buried, most of my time is spent in loungewear and T-shirts. As a thirty-two year old, I find I'd rather be comfortable than fashionable.

"I thought you read on your kindle? What's the point of all these books?"

"They're my trophies," I say, completely serious. "I read the ebook or listen to the audiobook, and then if I really liked it, I buy a physical copy for my shelves."

Jamie stares at me with a blank face, silently judging me. He'll be very excited about the bookshelves in storage I forgot to tell him about.

"Oh come on, give her a break."

My friend Joanna comes around the front of her truck carrying another box I forgot about labeled KITCHEN. After she reached out earlier this week, we've had a few conversations here and there via text. We tried to coordinate a time to get together, but she was busy all this week and I couldn't do anything this weekend because of the move. Out of nowhere, she offered to come help. I tried to convince her that was absolutely not necessary, but somehow she convinced me that she loves decorating. Eventually, I gave in so she could help me set up my bedroom while we caught up and had girl time. I did not expect her to be lifting my heavy boxes.

"Jo, you don't have to do that," I try to tell her for the third time.

She just shrugs and follows Jamie into the house.

"How else do you expect our dear little Raegan to escape

from this cruel, cruel world?" she continues, replying to Jamie's comment about my books.

I give her a grateful smile.

Jamie is smirking when I enter the living room. "Yes," he concedes, "but do we have space for all that escapism?"

"Of course," Jo responds. She sets the box down and gestures to the room around her. "Look at all this space. Plus, I bet you've got plenty of space in your room." She grins maniacally.

The banter may be at my expense, but seeing the two of them get along makes me happy.

We make our way up the stairs and Joanna spots a forgotten box of books by the stairs. "I've got it," she calls out, then follows Jamie and I up the steps to my bedroom.

Inside, I gently place a tote bag full of knick-knacks on the floor next to the stack of boxes Jamie has created. Instead of adding to it, Joanna drops her box on the bed.

I hear a massive *CRACK*, but before I can turn around, the damage has already been done. The bed frame has completely collapsed under the weight of the books, and the three of us stare flabbergasted at the now splintered wood protruding from underneath the mattress.

"Okay the books might actually be a problem," Joanna deadpans.

I'm too shocked to speak, so instead, I just stare at the disaster me and my books have caused.

Yet, when I sneak a glance at Jamie, he doesn't appear all that concerned. The exact opposite actually, he's laughing.

"What the hell is so funny?" Joanna demands. "I was about to apologize, but never-*fucking*-mind."

Jamie runs a hand over his face and rolls his eyes. "That bed was a hundred years old. It was my Nana's when she was a kid."

I knew this, but when Joanna and I glance at each other, thinking this detail should make the matter worse, Jamie starts laughing even harder.

After a moment, he manages to collect himself, hand splayed over his side as if clutching a stitch. "It was in storage after Nana died, but my mom insisted I put it in my guest room." A chuckle overcomes him again, and this time it's contagious. I can't help but fight a giggle as Jamie leans his head back and continues to laugh open-mouthed at the ceiling. "I told my mom it would break if someone breathed on it wrong. Turns out it was Raegan's smutty escapism."

I roll my eyes and cover my face in embarrassment. Beneath my fingers I mumble, "I've slept in this bed a dozen times."

"Yeah," Jamie concurs, "but you've never thrown your full weight on it like it's a trampoline."

Now all three of us are laughing, but Joanna suddenly stops, holding her hand in the air to halt us. "Wait," she starts. "Does that mean there's only one bed in this house?"

The realization hits before her punch line even lands. Jamie doesn't understand the significance, because he doesn't read romance, but now my stomach is in knots. At this very moment, a moving company is hauling the bed from my apartment to the thrift store. I briefly consider calling and telling them to turn around.

Taking a nap with Jamie in his bed is one thing, but if I have to sleep next to him every night, my brain might actually short circuit with too many lustful thoughts.

Whether or not I want to take things slow, the universe seems to have a different opinion.

"Okay, while you two sort out whatever that means," Jamie says, waving his hand between us, "I'm going to go grab your suitcase."

"Wait!" I squeak. "What about the bed?"

He shrugs his shoulders, unconcerned. "You don't need it."

What in the name of Romance-Tropes does that mean?

I SPEND the next few hours building my retrieved bookshelf in my new room and organizing all of my books by genre. After every book is put away, Joanna convinces me they'd look better in a rainbow pattern, so we spend another hour rearranging. After that, we move to the kitchen.

I'm happy to say that Jamie's agreement to let me bring all my lemon decor has not wavered. Yet. I'm not sure he realized just how much I have, but I'm sure when he sees how perfectly the yellow accents match with the sage green color of his walls, he won't mind.

As I unwrap my lemon-shaped fruit bowl, I spy a family of ghosts outside the window as they float down the street. They look to be taking a late afternoon stroll around the neighborhood, and I make a note to say hello the next time I see them. I'm not sure how acquainted Jamie is with his neighbors, but I will definitely be bringing them a potted plant to introduce myself. It's not like I can bake them cookies.

Joanna comes up next to me to investigate what I've been staring at, and it's then I notice the family has a dog—also a ghost. I wonder if it found the family after death or if they'd already been together in life.

"I have a pit like that at the rescue right now," Joanna tells me. "I wanted to spend time with her tomorrow and give her a bath, but I can't take the time I need with her when there's so much else to do."

"Do you have help?" I ask.

Joanna rolls her eyes dramatically. "I did, but two volunteers backed out on me earlier today. Teenagers: they're so lazy." She groans. "I'm so jealous."

"I can help," I offer. "It's the least I can do to repay you for helping me move."

Joanna's eyes go wide with equal parts shock and relief. "Really? You don't mind?"

I snicker. "Why would I mind spending the day with dogs?"

"Ahhh," she squeals, wrapping her arms around my middle and squeezing, "thank you, thank you!"

With my arms still pinned to my sides, I choke out a laugh. "What time do I need to be there?" I ask, trying to breathe.

Joanna finally lets go. "Just text me in the morning when you get up. Now," she claps her hands together readily, "I have to ask you something."

"Okay." I'm caught off guard by her sudden change in subject, but I'm curious what she's going to ask.

"Are you and Jamie hooking up?"

I almost drop the ceramic bowl in my hands. "What? Why would you think that?"

My visceral reaction only spurs her forward, and I wish I didn't wear my emotions on my sleeve. "Because you two very clearly have chemistry."

"We've been friends for years, Jo."

"Yes, I can see that. But I'm not talking about friendly chemistry. I'm talking about bedroom chemistry." If only she knew what we were doing on this counter yesterday. "All day he's been looking at you like he wants to eat you. And what the hell was the comment about you not needing a bed?"

"*Jo!*" I hiss under my breath, hoping Jamie isn't around to hear her.

"Okay, okay." She holds up both hands in surrender. "You don't have to tell me anything. He's cute, though." She winks.

"I would most definitely let him step on me if I was in your shoes."

"Jo." I don't exactly know what that means, but I get the general sentiment.

"Just know I'm a great listener when it comes to those sorts of things. You know," she winks again, more suggestively, "smutty things."

"Good to know," I mutter, finally placing the lemon bowl in the center of the kitchen table.

"You girls wanna grab dinner?" Jamie's deep baritone calls to us from the other room.

Joanna appears positively giddy. "Oh yeah, we can eat."

Eager to change the subject I yell back to Jamie, "Coming!" and Joanna nearly bursts from the seams with joy.

Chapter Twenty-Three

JAMIE

Later that evening, after Jo leaves, Raegan and I find ourselves alone.

We might be close—especially given how long I've known her—but watching her casually brush her teeth after making her come on my kitchen counter is a whole different level of intimate.

Not to mention, I've never lived with someone of the opposite sex that isn't related before.

I was properly educated on the female body at a young age, but not because of any sexual experience—I was a little late to the party on that front—but because my mom took the time to sit me down and explain the mechanics. She wanted me to know about a woman's menstrual cycle and understand that it was completely natural. This conversation came about after I'd found my sister's used tampon in the trash and thought her penis had fallen off.

Females are much less scary to me now in my thirties, but I'd be lying if I said the idea of sharing a bed with Raegan isn't a little intimidating. I've laid next to her as she fought off the remains of her anxiety, falling asleep on top of the covers while she's tucked safely under three layers of blankets. And yesterday I fell asleep with her curled into me, closer than we've ever been before. But that happened right after being intimate. Tonight, inches away from being skin to skin, we're expected to just...sleep?

Come on, Jamie. What're you so afraid of?

I'd already offered to sleep on the couch—I'm nothing if not chivalrous—and accepted the inevitable neck cramp that would come in the morning, but Raegan wouldn't have it. She still feels guilty for breaking the guest bed, despite my insistence that it wasn't a big deal. Though she tried to talk me into it, there was no way I was going to let her be the one to take the couch, so here we are.

If this happened a month ago, it wouldn't be so scary. Raegan has always felt like another sister—another confidant I can rely on. But things have changed so much in just one week. Our entire relationship has shifted into something so drastically different, I don't think I'll ever be able to look at her as anything else but *mine* ever again.

Raegan stands barefoot on the rug in my bedroom, her red toenail polish complimenting her pale skin. I've never been one to have a foot fetish, but Raegan's are so dainty and perfect, I'd be happy to kiss my way from the tip of her toes to the inside of her upper thigh. I could still smell the scent of her arousal lingering in the kitchen when I went to grab a bottle of water, and it nearly sent me into a frenzy.

She seems to have caught me staring, because her toes curl into the carpet. My eyes shoot back up to her face, but they don't miss her exposed thighs on the way up. She's wearing a pair of thin sleep shorts and a Shadow Hills Hobgoblins T-shirt: our high school mascot. It's one of hers this time, so it's more fitted.

"Are you sure you're okay with this?" she asks, crossing her arms and tucking her hands into her armpits. It looks like she's giving herself a hug, and it's adorable. But the way she's biting her lip is the farthest thing from adorable.

Why the hell did I have to notice the plumpness of her lips right before climbing into bed with her?

Cleetus appears with perfectly inconvenient timing, jumping jauntily to the bed with his tail curled into a question mark. His curiosity has driven him to explore the entirety of my condo today while Joanna and I hauled all of Raegan's things inside. Despite her claims of independence, Raegan can hardly open a soda bottle much less lift heavy boxes. And I don't fault her for it. It's always been my job to do any heavy lifting. Besides, her petite frame only lent itself to my benefit yesterday. Having her pressed against me, legs hooked around my waist, felt like a dream come true. Something I never knew I wanted but now I can't live without.

An ache starts to build in my balls, but I hastily shove all thoughts of fucking her far, far away and say, "I'm not going to eat you. Not unless you want me too."

I overheard the conversation between her and Jo earlier today, and I had to smother a laugh at her friend's comment about the way I'd apparently been staring at Raegan. But she wasn't wrong.

Cleetus then gives me a dirty look before finding a spot at the foot of the bed to start making his evening biscuits, and I wonder awkwardly if he's able to sense the shift between us as well.

I lift the edge of the comforter and slip underneath, relishing the cool touch of the blanket on my skin. Raegan follows my lead and shifts her weight a few times before settling. She's on her back, eyes staring at the ceiling as her fingers grip the edge of the comforter and pull it up to her chin.

"Rae," I say her name quietly. "We don't have to do anything else."

The silence is thicker than the saliva that's built up on my tongue. I swallow, needing to get this out, because I don't want her to feel like hooking up again is mandatory just because it happened once.

"I don't expect anything," I tell her honestly. "Whatever you're comfortable with is what I want. Mates or not, it's always your decision."

She waits a moment before responding. Then I hear her quietly say, "Thank you."

The awkward silence is broken when her foot accidentally bumps Cleetus on the head and he *meows* in offense.

"Sorry, sweet boy," she apologizes, lifting her head to make sure he's alright. The beast settles into a ball against her calf and lets out a dramatic sigh.

"I don't remember giving him permission to sleep in the bed." I say it jokingly, but I'm not *not* serious.

She relaxes. "He doesn't need permission."

"No he doesn't," I grumble, rolling my eyes. On cue, the cat growls low in his throat, and I can feel the vibration in my feet.

"I did say we're a package deal."

I sit up and look him straight in his yellow eyes. "And that's the only reason you're here." He doesn't bother with a response. As I lay back down, I reach to turn off the light. "Goodnight, Rae."

She murmurs a goodnight back to me, and then we're in the dark.

Chapter Twenty-Four

RAEGAN

Being this close to Jamie is like standing too close to an open flame. His body heat alone feels like it's going to burn me alive, and his smell is far too intoxicating for me to think straight. Being in his room, that sweet musky scent is sending my sense of smell into overdrive. This is the second time I've been in his bed in as many days, surrounded by his freakin' pheromones and masculine energy. Yesterday, I was relaxed and in a post-orgasm coma, so drifting off was easy. But now, I'm wound up tighter than a wire, and I'm not sure how I'll ever be able to fall asleep.

"Why don't you have a top sheet?" I ask quietly, trying to distract my mind from the feel of Jamie's thigh merely an inch from mine.

I feel him shift to his side. "I get hot when I sleep so one layer is plenty." A beat of silence passes, and I know he's thinking about whether or not he should go get an extra blanket. "Do you want one? I can find something for you."

"No, Jamie. I don't need to be a burrito every night."

He rolls to his back again, satisfied with my answer. This

overprotective nature of his might end up feeling a bit grating if it becomes too constant, but I can admit it feels nice to be looked after.

I'm on my back as well, but I can tell from the corner of my eye as I adjust to the darkness that he's watching me. I wonder if he's thought about my lips the way I've been thinking about his all day.

I keep fidgeting absentmindedly, then after adjusting my sleep shorts for the fourth time, I finally stop moving, but I'm far from settled.

His voice softly fills the quiet. "If you do decide you want to be a burrito, just let me know."

His desire to take care of me smothers any flame of annoyance I might have like a blanket over a fire. Because that's what Jamie is: my security blanket. Only right now, rather than feeling comforted by his presence, everything from his smell to the sound of his breathing threatens to smother me. But in a good way—a *holy-shit-please-just-step-on-me* kinda way, like Joanna would say.

Each second that passes in the darkness takes a lifetime, and my anxious mind thrives off of it. My racing thoughts hop from one scenario to the next like lily pads, reliving every moment of the past two days. Like the feel of Jamie's rough hands on my thigh, how wet I was for him from just the sound of his words in my ear. But before I can lose myself in the erotic memory, my mind jumps to the moment I watched him run off into the woods with the rest of his pack. It feels like a lifetime ago when I first learned about the colossal secret he's been keeping and saw him in his wolf form for the first time, yet it's only been two days.

I remember running back to my car in sopping wet clothes and a snotty nose. At that moment, it didn't matter that I felt like a drowned rat sitting in the driver's seat. My heart felt so full, it propelled me throughout the drive home. But after making it to his house, surrounded by all of his things, I felt extremely lonely.

Though I've finally convinced myself to accept his offer to move in, I know it's going to take a while for this place to truly feel like home. I can only hope that being with Jamie will help ease the transition. Because despite so much change, he's here. And he's still mine. More so now than ever before.

It's hard for me to imagine being someone's mate. Being tethered to them in such a permanent way seems foreboding. But the romance reader in me also finds it incredibly romantic. I've read books about fated mates before, in fairy tales and fantastical worlds, but not in real life. Not like this. It's common knowledge that werewolves have mates, but instead of reading about it in books, I'm living it. I'm a romance heroine come to life.

The longer I lay in the dark listening to Jamie's steady breaths, intrusive thoughts start telling me things I don't want to hear.

Being his mate means he's going to be stuck with you.

He's going to get sick of you.

He's going to resent you.

I groan and roll over to face away from Jamie. The wall of his bedroom is illuminated by the faint glow of the waning moon. Its current phase holds no claim over him, but in a few weeks, he'll be forced to shift again. I wonder what it is about that he despises so much. Is it painful? Is it scary? It must be, losing yourself to a different state of mind, one you won't even remember.

And what is it like, being in a body that's not human? Will he get sick from being in the rain all night even though he had a different set of sinuses at the time? Is his fur thick enough to have kept him warm?

"I can hear you worrying over there."

Jamie's voice startles me. "I am not."

"You are," he deadpans.

Then I feel his hand on my arm. He rubs up and down, bringing goosebumps to my skin, but it's soothing. The bed sinks as his weight shifts and then he's right behind me, holding me just like he did yesterday after our kiss, after he explored me for the first time. It's the feel of his body pressed to mine that eventually shuts off my mind, allowing me to sleep peacefully.

Chapter Twenty-Five

JAMIE

The moment Raegan's alarm goes off on her phone Saturday morning, she bolts out of bed and rushes to the guest bathroom to take a shower. Her absence from the bed immediately hits me as I roll onto my stomach and moan into her pillow. The smell of her coconut shampoo fills my nostrils, soothing the ache in my chest that has swelled from her absence.

We'll be getting a new bed frame for her room today, which means last night might have been my last opportunity to share a bed with Raegan Baker. We still have so much to discuss, and having time to think over the whole 'being mates' situation, she might very well turn and run in the opposite direction.

I want her to take as long as she needs, but what if Rhett was right about your soul eventually giving up if you ignore the pull for too long? What if, by the time she decides she wants to be together, the fire between us has fizzled out? There are so many layers to the situation now. Last week, all I wanted was for her to move in with me, but what if she eventually changes her mind about that too?

I'll just have to savor her scent in my sheets for as long as it lingers.

I take my time dragging myself out from under the blanket, giving Raegan plenty of hot water before starting my own shower. After I hear the water cease to run through the pipes, I strip from my boxers and turn the knob in the shower to freezing, because yes, after having Raegan's ass pressed against my groin all night, my balls are bluer than the walls of this room.

I wash quickly, my body shaking violently from the temperature, and when I'm done, I stand naked on the plush rug staring at my reflection in the fogged up mirror.

How did we get here?

I have to stop this dangerous way of thinking. She's already made it clear she wants me, but I can't let that drive my actions. I will give her whatever time she needs, even if she doesn't want it. Because in the end, I don't want there to be a single ounce of possibility that she might regret anything between us.

After the incident with Patrick, it felt like something in me snapped. It wasn't just that I wanted to protect Raegan from someone that would cause her harm, at that moment, I needed to shelter her from the entire world. I needed to pull her into my arms and claim her as mine because, with me by her side, no one would ever think about hurting her. Ever again.

Now I've accepted the reality of what happened—that moment with Patrick being the spark that ignited the mate bond between us—I thought that extreme need would fade. I understand it now, the raw, primal desire to claim and protect. Yet the more time passes, the stronger that desire gets. I'm finding that fighting against this bond is an even tougher battle than fighting the shift each month, and that's saying something.

After getting dressed, I find Raegan in the kitchen, pouring coffee into a travel mug. Her dark hair is still wet from the shower, and she hasn't brushed it out yet. Thick clumps of knotted waves fall to the top of her shoulders and drip water onto her maroon sweatshirt. She's wearing stretchy black biker shorts, her porcelain legs on display, and I want nothing more than to spread those pretty thighs apart on the kitchen table and have her for breakfast.

Instead, I clear my throat. "What're your plans this morning?"

She glances up as I enter the room, fresh-faced and makeup free. I love the way she looks without makeup. I love her with it, too. But without the mascara and photoshopped complexion, she's the girl I've known since high school.

The girl I want to spend the rest of my life with.

"I promised I'd help Joanna at the rescue today," she says, placing a lid on her cup. "I'll text you when we're done, and then we can go to the furniture store."

My heart sinks. I was being completely serious yesterday when I told her she didn't need a bed. But I guess she still wants her space.

"Okay. Just remember," I say, making sure my voice is clear of any emotion, "Cleetus likes being an only child." I nod toward the loaf of fur on the back of the couch. As if agreeing with me, he lifts his head and gives Raegan a slow blink.

Her face turns into that of a doting mother and she rushes to give him a kiss on the forehead. "No siblings today, I promise," she mews, telling him more than me. "You're still my number one baby boy."

I can hear him purring from where I'm standing across the room. He's a baby alright–a spoiled one.

"How many dogs does she have now ?" I ask, moving to the refrigerator to grab a carton of oatmilk.

As I prepare my own cup of coffee, Raegan continues peppering Cleetus with kisses. She finally stops and turns for the door.

"I think ten?" She says it as if she's not really sure. "Jo said a family dropped off a pitbull a few days ago. It was 'too aggressive' with their newborn," she says with air quotes.

No doubt the family simply doesn't want to take the time to train a young dog, or they hadn't paid attention to the animal's personality traits when adopting. Some dogs just need to overcome their trauma. Other dogs just need to get out their energy, and I have a feeling a couple with a newborn doesn't have the time or energy necessary to take care of, essentially, another child.

"Then there were three found abandoned on a farm last week," Raegan continues. "They were tied up and left outside, so they need extra affection and human interaction."

"So when you say 'helping', what you're really saying is you're going to play with a bunch of dogs." Raegan smiles sheepishly. I move to plant a gentle kiss on her forehead. "Have fun."

Her smile turns unabashed.

And with that, she's out the door, leaving me alone with Cleetus. He doesn't bother glancing my way. He simply tucks his head between his paws and goes back to sleep.

Chapter Twenty-Six

RAEGAN

Jo's rescue is located about half a mile past the werewolf pack's territory. It sits on the edge of the forest, tucked into a section of trees that surround the property. Two large barns, outfitted with playrooms, bathing areas, and a clinic, sit on the western side of the farm. On the eastern side is the main building, and pushing back into the forest is an open area of paddocks and farm land stretching for about ten acres. Besides running a rescue for abandoned dogs, and sometimes cats, she also takes care of three cows, two horses, one pig, one turtle, and six chickens.

I head straight for the barns and find Jo dragging out a plastic kiddie pool. It kicks up dust as it slides across the bumpy dirt lot and settles with a *poof* when she drops it into place.

"Hey!" Jo greets me, hands on her hips. She's wearing a pair of dark rounded sunglasses, and her brown hair, a shade or two lighter than mine, is plaited into two long braids that drape over her shoulders. A red bandana is tied around her head like a headband, the bow resting above her right ear. She's wearing a pair of tan cargo pants with about a dozen pockets and a cropped navy crewneck. She looks like she's ready to paint a house, or maybe plant some flowers.

Before I can say anything, two large dogs bound from the barn and start circling Joanna. They pounce and wag their tails happily, eager for whatever it is they think is happening.

"Sorry, guys," Jo tells them. "This isn't for you." The lab with short black fur and floppy ears lets out a sad but adorable whine, and the other, a brown-colored mix with pointed ears, sits without command, then huffs out a breath of air when it doesn't gain him anything. Joanna looks at me. "These two love B.A.T.H. time." She spells it out so the balls of energy nipping at her heels don't understand her, then narrows her eyes on them while still directing her next statement at me. "But they already had their time in the sprinklers yesterday."

The brown mix then proceeds to roll onto his back and wiggle, purposefully coating his fur in dried leaves and dirt.

I let out a laugh. "He's smart."

"Too smart." Joanna groans then commands, "Get up, Moose." He snaps to attention, ears perked and waiting to see if his plan has worked. It hasn't.

She points a finger to the barn. "Go inside." Slowly, he moseys back inside. "You too, Thumper." The black lab just looks confused, but listens to the command nonetheless.

"You've got some characters," I say.

"Those two are nothing compared to the princess you're about to meet."

My heart swells as I follow Jo into the larger barn. I've been looking forward to spending time here since agreeing to help yesterday afternoon, but not only because of the chance to spend time with adorable animals. As I wrestled to sleep last night, lying next to Jamie, I realized I don't have anyone to talk to about everything that's happened. If this were any other situation, I would go to Jamie, but for obvious reasons that's not an option. I've never truly confided in Joanna before, but right now I really need another woman's advice. Afterall, she told me herself that she's a great listener, so I want to take her up on that.

She leads me to the back of the building where there are two rows of spacious kennels, each with a lattice fence serving as a door. The moment we approach, I expect to be met with enthusiastic barks and the sound of paws tapping against the barriers, but it's mostly quiet, other than the sound of mouths scarfing food from bowls. It seems I arrived just after breakfast was served.

At the end of the first row, in kennel number five, is the small pit bull Joanna mentioned being the newest resident. She's a mix of tan and white and has the cutest little rolls I've seen in my life. I lean over the door to let her sniff me and after hesitating for only a few seconds she starts licking the inside of my arm.

"She's so sweet," I coo. "What made those people think she was aggressive?"

"I'm pretty sure all she did was bark a little too loudly at their baby, but I have no doubt it was warranted. Children are way more unpredictable than dogs. The baby probably screamed all day and she was just trying to scream along with it."

I can feel Joanna's frustration. Taking care of abandoned animals is a hard job, especially when you have to face the humans that do it and keep a professional manner. I'm sure Jo has had to fight the urge to punch people like that on more than one occasion.

The pit bumps her head against my hand signaling for me to pet her, so I scratch the top of her head.

"If you can't properly take care of a dog, then don't get one," Joanna declares. "She just needs training, that's all." I wholeheartedly agree. "They named her Lucy, but she doesn't really respond to it, so I'm going to start calling her Juno."

"Why Juno?" I ask.

Joanna smiles down at the dog. "Because I'm gonna treat her like a queen."

I SPEND the next hour letting Juno warm up to me before giving her a bath. I take her on a long walk around the perimeter of the rescue, letting her stop and smell everything that peaks her interest. With such a round body and short legs, she has to move quickly to keep up with my longer stride, but that doesn't stop her from darting ahead and attacking piles of leaves whenever they seem to offend her.

After I'm sure she's gotten out her energy and we've formed a good connection, I take her back to the barn into one of the bathing rooms. Joanna has a station already set up with all the tools we'll need. I adjust the knobs to the perfect temp and fill the tub with about four inches of water, then I coax Juno into the bath. To my surprise, she jumps in willingly, excited to splash about. I scrub her down and rinse, moisturize her nose and paws, and add a fresh smelling dog safe perfume to her fur. When we're all done, she looks happy and sleepy, so I take her back to her room so she can take a nap.

By the time I'm done, Joanna enters the barn after finishing whatever tasks that have kept her busy. There are a few strands of straw in her hair and she reaches to pick them out as she asks, "How did it go?"

"Juno was great. We really bonded over our shared love of stopping to smell the flowers. And leaves. And the grass."

Jo coughs out a laugh. "I knew she'd be great. She's a sweetheart. I'm so tired of people labeling puppies as difficult simply because they are puppies." She looks toward Juno's stall thoughtfully. "I have a bunch of leftover charcuterie board shit at the house if you feel like sticking around a bit longer."

"That sounds fantastic."

I follow her to the main house and up the steps. She leads me to a large farmhouse style kitchen complete with a massive sink and exposed hardware. Jo places crackers, cheese, a mix of veggies, and a jar of olives on the counter, and we both assemble our own snack plates. I make mini cucumber sandwiches with cream cheese and buttery crackers, and we sit in comfortable silence for a few minutes while we eat.

I decide now is as good a time as any to have that heart to heart. But before I can open my mouth to say anything, Joanna speaks up first.

"Listen, I'm sorry for being so pushy about you and Jamie yesterday."

Her apology is unnecessary, but based on the look she's giving me, she seems to be genuinely concerned about upsetting me.

"You don't need to apologize," I tell her.

"Yes I do. I thought about how I acted on the way home, and I realized I might have made you a little uncomfortable," she admits. "I don't know the situation between you two, so it's not my place to joke about it. I just thought you guys fit so well together, and...I don't know." She shrugs in defeat and pops an olive unceremoniously into her mouth.

"It's okay. I swear." *Here goes nothing.* "If I'm being completely honest," I say, "you were right."

Jo's ears perk up and she tilts her head. "I was?"

"Things between Jamie and I have changed recently, and we hooked up for the first time the other day." I rush on before I lose my courage, "He kinda got me off on the kitchen counter and now things are weird and I don't want them to be weird and I'm not sure what to do."

"Wait, *kinda?*"

It's not the first question I thought she'd ask, but I should have been more clear about that part.

"Sorry, he did," I clarify, stumbling over my words. "He definitely did the job. Great job. Five stars."

Jo doesn't react, only gives me a blank stare.

"What?"

"Oh nothing. It's just, for someone whose best friend since high school just touched their pussy for the first time, you were acting like it was a normal Saturday."

"Well I didn't want to bring it up first thing in the morning."

"Why not?" she demands, smacking her palm flat on the counter for emphasis. "That's very important information. You should be screaming about it!"

Her bluntness nails my reaction to this entire situation on the head. I haven't known how to act when it comes to this new dynamic between Jamie and me. I think I've subconsciously been trying to keep everything the same, but that's not the reality of the situation. If we're going to move forward, I have to embrace the change.

So I tell her the truth.

"I'm afraid to start something serious," I confess, "because if we break up, I'll lose him as my friend."

Jo nods sympathetically and reaches her hand across the counter to take mine. "First of all, that's stupid. From what I know about Jamie, even if he hated you, he would never leave your side." She pats the top of my hand with her other and adds, "Besides, you have me."

It makes me sad that I never gave Jo enough credit. All this time I let a great friendship go to waste, simply because I never thought to confide in her. Though I wish I could have realized sooner, I'm happy I have her now.

I smile and give her hand a light squeeze.

"I think you just have to trust the connection you already have," she says. "If something is going to happen between you, it will happen naturally. Don't let yourself feel embarrassed or scared just because he's your friend. If anything, that should make you feel more comfortable with each other."

I hadn't thought of it that way before, but she has a point.

"And if you do decide to go forward with it," she adds, "just think of it like taking a car for a test drive. Take him for a ride, girl. And I'm going to need all the details."

Chapter Twenty-Seven

JAMIE

It's around 3:30 in the afternoon when I hear Raegan come in through the front door. I've been ready and waiting for her to get back for the past hour, but as she comes into the kitchen, I make myself look busy on my laptop. I continue replying to a nonexistent email as she sits down at the table and wipes sweat from her forehead. Her sweatshirt looks damp, either from sweat or something else I don't want to know about.

"That took a little longer than expected," she sighs, apology lacing her voice.

"No worries." I make a show of closing my laptop. "You've got perfect timing. I just finished up."

The lie comes a little too easily, but the relief on her face makes it worth it.

"Just let me go change real quick," she says before darting back to her bedroom. It hasn't sunken in yet that it's officially hers.

I wait patiently with my keys already in hand while she changes. When she steps back into the kitchen, she's wearing a long sleeve black shirt and loose-fitting jeans. Her hair has been readjusted from a high bun on top of her head to a low ponytail. She's flushed, cheeks pink as she rolls her sleeves up to her elbows. "Well, what are we waiting for?" Her smirk makes my heart thump as I follow her out of the door, locking up behind us.

THE CLOSEST FURNITURE store is about thirty minutes outside of town. As we make our way to the highway, I try my best to keep my eyes on the road, but I'm finding it hard to look away from Raegan. She insisted we roll the windows down to enjoy the cool breeze, and now she's got one hand extended outside the cab to catch the air in her spread fingers. Small strands of hair fly wildly around her face, eyes closed. Like this, she appears innocent and unmarred, and I want to keep this image of her in my mind forever.

I can see splotches of greenish yellow starting to form amidst the purple bruising on her neck, meaning it's finally beginning to heal. Throughout this entire week since the attack, I don't think she's made a single effort to hide it. The sentiment makes me proud, because I know her decision to show it is brave. It's her small way of choosing to stay in the open instead of hiding herself away.

When we finally reach the furniture store, the first thing Raegan does is get distracted by a set of lemon themed serving trays. I have to physically take her by the shoulders and steer her in the opposite direction.

"No more lemon shit," I insist.

"I thought we agreed you weren't going to call me that."

I wink at her suggestively. "You're right. Just lemon."

Her cheeks go pink again, but this time I know my use of her new nickname is what's made her overheat. I hadn't actually planned on using it regularly, but seeing the way it's made her squirm each time it comes out of my mouth has made it all the more enjoyable.

Still, I don't want it to become like one of those cutesy pet names, so instead, I plan to use it only for special occasions. That way she knows exactly what it means. And it seems I've done my job, given how hard she's currently avoiding eye contact with me.

We browse the bedroom section of the store, looking for the right size and style that Raegan is looking for. The guest room isn't super spacious, so if we're being realistic, a full size frame would be best, but I want her to have a comfortable space just like the one she had in her old room, so we opt for the queen.

The frame she ultimately picks out has a simple wrought iron headboard with swirling filigree around the top of each rod. Undoubtedly, the first thought that comes to mind when I see it is the image of Raegan's hands gripping the bars while I'm pounding into her from behind.

Clearly, our tryst in the kitchen was *not* enough to dull the constant ache in my balls I've felt for two days straight.

Secretly, I wonder if the image has crossed her mind as well. Because although the style is fitting of her preference, I swear she smirks as she grabs the attention of the nearest employee and points to her choice.

AFTER WE GET HOME, it takes two hours for us to put together the bed frame due to my insistence of not needing the instructions. Of course, Raegan proved me wrong when the piece I thought I'd screwed together properly was actually missing three more bolts and fell apart the moment I let go. Begrudgingly, I allowed her to walk me through the rest of the steps until finally, a completed frame sat neatly against the back wall of Raegan's new bedroom.

Together we hauled the mattress from the hallway back into her room and placed it strategically on top of the iron slats, though I would say I probably carried ninety percent of the weight. Then Raegan took her time adding the sheets and dressing the duvet with her fluffy pillows and favorite throw blanket.

After the project was finished, we both stood back to admire our handy work. I reflected back her satisfied grin, but inside I felt a little bittersweet about the situation. The other day felt like we had finally started something, and now, it's like we're taking a step backward, erasing the progress we've made.

"I'll let you finish organizing," I say, wiping sweat from my brow with the back of my forearm.

Leaving her to one of her favorite past times, I head downstairs to grab a glass of water and relax on the couch. I flip on the TV to whatever football game is currently on and stretch out along the corner of the sectional.

Surely watching my favorite sport will be enough to distract me from the nagging thoughts in my brain. But it's proving rather difficult, no matter how hard I try to focus on the players running across my screen.

An hour or so passes, and eventually I find myself actually tuned in to the game. It's been a close score throughout the fourth quarter, and I'm waiting to see if the team that's down by one point is going to go for the two-point conversion. But just as they start to line up for the next play, I'm caught off guard by a very prominent scent.

I look up and spot Raegan coming down the stairs. She's got her earbuds in, and she's changed into a pair of slouchy lounge pants and a different sweatshirt than the one she wore this morning. This one is blue with lyrics from one of her favorite singers. It matches her eyes, but that's not what I'm focused on. Right now, my entire set of predatory senses is lasered in on the very clear scent of arousal that's wafting from her.

What the hell has she been doing up there?

Then I put it together. She's been listening to an audiobook while organizing her room, and something tells me she's at a particularly spicy part in the story.

She walks past the entryway that leads to the living room and goes straight to the refrigerator in the kitchen, making a point not to look in my direction. I watch her knowingly as she fills her water cup and takes a long, desperate sip.

I have two options here: either I can choose to ignore that she's very clearly turned on by whatever she's reading and go back to watching the game I now have no interest in, *or*...I can offer my assistance. It would be the gentlemanly thing to do. Not to mention, if I hear the buzz of a vibrator after she goes back upstairs, I might actually lose my shit.

The smell of her arousal takes me right back to the moment I had her perched atop the counter she's now facing, and my cock starts to swell.

Fuck it.

I decide to go with my primal instincts and just go for it, praying she doesn't turn me down. I need this last opportunity. I need one more chance to watch her fall apart from my touch. Because if this is all I get—if I never get to kiss her soft lips or feel her silky smooth skin beneath my fingers ever again—at least I'll have the memory of this moment.

I take my time walking into the kitchen, playing out a scenario in which I'm just casually going for a snack in the pantry. Raegan keeps her back to me, very clearly trying to avoid eye contact. I open the pantry door and rummage around, making a show of crinkling a bag of chips, then I close it. She hasn't moved, but I can see she's carefully opening a sleeve of crackers.

My hand grips the edge of the counter where her pretty pussy had been on display for me only two days ago. She senses my presence and turns around, finally making eye contact with me. Mine must be wild with lust, because she lets out a soft gasp.

"Don't tell me that book you're listening to is what's got you smelling so sweet."

Chapter Twenty-Eight

RAEGAN

My mouth immediately goes dry. I forgot he can smell...everything.

Jamie's eyes are dark with desire, the typical warm brown color fading to that of a midnight sky.

"I can help you with that," he says, voice lower than usual. Those dark eyes dart to my thighs as I press them tightly together.

I paused the current chapter of my book before coming down the stairs, needing a break from the intensely descriptive cunnilingus scene I'd just listened to. The spice scene snuck up on me while putting away the last of my clothes into drawers, and without realizing it, instead of picturing the book's love interest with his face between the main character's legs, I was very clearly picturing Jamie.

"What's it about?" he asks.

"W-what?"

"The book," he clarifies. "What is the book about?"

I nervously play with the plastic wrapping I just pulled from a pack of crackers. I'd come downstairs for a snack, and a bit of a breather, but now I don't feel all that hungry anymore.

"It's a romance," I tell him sheepishly.

He grins wickedly and takes a step forward. "Can I listen?"

I want to say no, but what is there to hide? He already knows what it is, and definitely knows what it's done to me. I slip one of my earbuds out and hand it to him tentatively. After he places it in ear, I double tap the other to signal playback.

I stand painfully still while the scene continues to play out in both our ears. I'm listening to the same words he is, so whenever his right hand grips the counter just a little bit tighter, I know exactly which part made him do so.

After what feels like an agonizing five minutes, he removes the ear bud and hands it back to me. "Sounds like he knows what he's doing."

My gaze drops to the floor. I'm too embarrassed to meet his eyes. There's not a doubt in my mind that Jamie would know what he's doing in that category. Based solely on the skill of his hands, I think his mouth could definitely hold its own.

As if reading my mind, he takes my chin in his fingers and lifts my face so I'm looking at him once more. "I bet I could do better."

My breath hitches. "Jamie."

Now he's flush against me, right back in the same spot we were before.

Hearing him speak to me in such a provocative manner rattles me. I want to hear more of it, but at the same time my body naturally wants to shy away from his crude words. I've never been spoken to like this before, not like the men I read about in my books.

"What is it, lemon?" he asks gently, lowering his hand to stroke the tender skin along the column of my neck. "Does it make you uncomfortable, me talking about pleasuring you?"

I shake my head. It's not that his words make me uncomfortable. I'm just nervous, and I'm unsure how to act when we're slowly crossing these boundaries one by one. This is my sweet friend, Jamie—the one who has seen me cry, laughed with me, laughed at me, the man whose hug feels like home. Now that same friend is talking to me in a language I've never heard before.

A language I could get used to.

Jamie's forehead drops to mine, and I watch through lowered lashes as his shoulders rise and fall, breathing me in. I wish I knew what my scent smelled like to him. Being human, my olfaction abilities are abysmal compared to his. While I can take simple pleasure in his musky smell of maple and damp soil, Jamie is able to bask in every molecule of *me*. I can't imagine what that must be like.

His mouth moves slowly to the shell of my ear as he whispers, "You never need to feel uncomfortable or embarrassed with me, Raegan." Then he pulls away to meet my eyes. "I just want to take care of you. Whether it's going bed shopping or being there when you're anxious." He removes his other hand from the counter and traces a line beneath my sweatshirt starting at my hip and up my waist, then trailing beneath my breast. "Or simply making you feel good." Everything Jamie does makes me feel good. "Do you want me to do that for you?"

I'm not wearing a bra, so my eyes flutter closed when his thumb grazes my peaked nipple. I hear the tell-tale growl in the back of his throat, meaning he's waiting to pounce. I've never had a man go down on me before—the act has always felt a bit too intimate for a non-serious relationship—but after picturing what was being read to me by the narrators of my spicy audiobook, I want Jamie to do it.

There's part of me that worries the farther we go with this, the farther we'll get from what we were, but then I remember what Joanna told me. No matter what happens between Jamie and me, there's no scenario in which I lose him as a friend. It's going to take time figuring out this new dynamic between us, so why not have fun while I do? Take that test drive.

"Jamie." I breathe his name in as I fill my lungs with air then release it slowly.

"Yes."

"Make me feel good."

The command hits his mark, but he doesn't immediately start ravishing me like before. Instead, he takes my hand and guides me to the living room. I follow obediently, and when he gestures for me to sit on the couch, I do so eagerly.

He kneels to the floor and hooks his fingers around the waistbands of my pants and underwear. "Can I take these off?"

I nod and lift my hips. The pants are loose and come off easily as he drags the soft, stretchy material over my hips and down my legs.

Though I'm still not used to being completely bare to him, I'm less unsure than the first time. Now I understand the authenticity behind his desire to take care of me. He truly means it in every sense of the word, and I think I've officially decided to let him.

His mouth moves to my inner thigh and I shudder at the feel of his lips on such sensitive skin. His fingers had been enough to nearly drive me insane, so how am I going to survive his mouth on me? I need to concentrate on something else or I might become overstimulated too quickly, so I grab at the collar of his shirt. "Take this off."

Jamie looks up at me with wild eyes. "Yes ma'am."

He grabs the back of his shirt collar and yanks it over his head seamlessly, leaving me with the stunning view of his shoulder muscles as he leans back down into position between my thighs. He doesn't ask me to remove my sweatshirt, and I'm grateful. I don't think I'm quite ready to be completely naked in front of him.

"Spread those pretty legs for me, lemon."

There's no room for interpretation with that nickname. It's not cute or teasing. It sounds lustful and completely focused, but that might be because he's currently perched between my legs and ready to devour me like his favorite dessert.

I heed his command, eager to feel something besides the cool air against my wet core. Jamie lifts one of my legs over his shoulder and starts by sliding his hand from the back of my knee to the apex of my thighs, his eyes following the journey. When his thumb reaches the wetness surrounding my clit, I bite my bottom lip. He glides through my lips, thumb coated in my arousal just like before, only this time he doesn't dip inside me. He takes his time tracing the contours of my body. Finally, he meets my eyes with a wild hunger, and I brace myself.

His lips are featherlight at first—a gentle touch to ease me into the feel of them. Then his tongue darts out and licks from bottom to top. The sensation is incomparable. It feels good, but it's too subtle. In order to truly feel pleasure, I need the opposite. I need firm, deliberate pressure.

I squirm under him, teetering along the line of uncomfortable sensitivity. Jamie clearly knows I've never done this before, but instead of going about his business and ignoring my nonverbal cues, he stops.

"What do you need?"

I adjust my hips so I'm slanted further into the couch, giving him better access. "It's too soft."

His tongue darts out to lick my wetness from his lips and the corner of his mouth turns up in a knowing smirk. I hope he isn't about to make fun of me.

"Don't worry," he says, his eyes appearing almost iridescent, alight with desire. "I know what you need."

He takes both hands and grabs my ass to hold me in place. This time when his tongue carves its path, he doesn't just lick, he presses down firmly, and *this* ignites a sensational flutter in my stomach muscles.

One of my hands finds its way to the soft strands of his hair, while the other grips the couch. When he reaches my clit, he sucks with his whole mouth and my hips buck involuntarily, but his hands hold me steady and force me back in place. The harder his tongue works the harder it is to keep my thighs apart, and I want so badly to press them together and ride that insatiable ache that's building in my core.

I need something solid to grind against, and as much as I'm loving the feel of his tongue pressing into my clit, it's not enough. Instinctively, he slides two fingers into my heat, filling the empty ache that's lingered there.

As much as it feels good, I want to grab him and pull him to me. I want to feel the weight of him on top of me. He's created a rhythm that my body is following, and the beginnings of an orgasm have started to build deep beneath the surface, but it's going to take more than this to finish it.

Somehow, Jamie already knows my body like the palm of his own hand, because that's what he's using now to press firmly against my clit, rubbing endless circles until I'm panting and clenching my thighs together. He gets up from the floor and perches a knee on the cushions beside me, his free hand moving to the back of the couch to hold himself steady while still maintaining the same circling pressure between my legs.

He navigates me through the height of my orgasm, up, up, up, until his lips meet mine, and I can taste myself on his tongue.

I'm still spiraling as he slows his movements. Yet again, I

am undone by this man, and I don't even know where to start when it comes to the daunting task of putting myself back together.

Chapter Twenty-Nine

JAMIE

I don't know what I was thinking.

I'll never be satisfied when it comes to Raegan. Every memory I create with her shuddering beneath me in pleasure only pushes me to create more. There are too many ways I want to coax an orgasm from her and appreciate that expression she made: mouth open, head tilted back, and eyes closed. She looked like a goddess experiencing heaven for the first time. And there's no way in hell I'll ever be able to go without seeing that look on her face again.

I go to the downstairs bathroom and grab a towel for Raegan to clean off with. She stays where she is on the couch with her thighs apart, pussy glistening and swollen. For a split second, I think about leaving her there to look at while I take care of the excruciating hard on I've been sporting since the moment I realized what she was listening to. But I'm not that guy—not unless she asks me to be.

When I return with a damp towel, Raegan's eyes are still glossy with want, and I almost question whether or not she climaxed, but she definitely did.

She takes the towel and wipes herself carefully, all the while keeping her eyes on the bulge in my sweatpants. I can't be sure, but I think she might want to continue what we started.

"You haven't let me touch you yet," she notes, doe-like eyes trained on the exact area she's referring to.

I grin, feeling like a teenager again.

She grabs her bikini-like underwear from the floor and slips them on, then she moves to stand directly in front of me. I'm still shirtless, so she takes the opportunity to run the dark red nail of her index finger down my left peck. I imagine one of those nails gripping my cock, and it feels like I'm running a temperature again.

But I can't.

I take her hand and kiss her palm. "Raegan." I say her name lovingly, and she instantly registers the lack of seduction in my tone.

She pulls back. "You don't want me to?"

"Of course I want you to," I rush. "I told you, it's yours whenever you want. But if you do this now, I don't think I'll be able to hold back from going further."

She swallows, and I watch the muscles of her throat work. My imagination runs wild, but I reel it back in.

"I want to go further," she says with determination.

With her half naked in front of me, still smelling like sex, I'm finding it really hard to remember why we can't.

I cup her cheek and pull her flush against my chest, wrapping my other arm around her waist. "I want to have sex with you, Rae. I really do. But there are things you need to know before we do."

Her breath blows softly against my cheek as she asks, "What things?"

I guess we're having this conversation now.

I have to force myself to think clearly. Because right now her arousal is clouding the air and frying my wolfy brain cells. My human ones, too.

I take a deep breath, then guide us back to the couch, only this time I sit beside her. She grabs one of the pillows and hugs it, preparing for whatever I have to say.

"If we were to have sex, that would mean you've officially accepted the mate bond. It's a physical way of sealing the deal, so to speak, but there are certain things that happen the first time we do it."

Raegan is looking at me quizzically. I can tell she's interested in learning more, but she's also a little scared. "Do you have to bite me or something?"

"No. That's vampires." I laugh, then gather my next words carefully. "That pull between us, it feels like a rope connecting us together, right?"

"Uh huh."

"Well, having sex would...tie a knot."

She scrunches her nose. "Like getting married?"

"No." My face now feels like it's on fire. "It's more of a literal knot than a metaphorical one."

Based on the look on her face, she has no clue what I'm talking about. Unfortunately, I probably won't be able to explain it any better with my hormones and wolfish instincts all jumbled together.

I rub my temples. "Jesus, I can barely think straight with you sitting here like that, your taste still on my tongue." I close my eyes to hide what is most definitely a smirk from Raegan, take a deep breath, and continue, "All you need to know right now is that having sex means the bond is permanent." The tension in my skull eases, so I place a hand on her thigh. "I just want you to be a thousand percent certain that's what you want before that happens. Alright?"

I watch as her tense posture finally loosens. "I understand," she finally says. "Thank you."

Happy with where this difficult conversation has ended, I pull her to me and she falls lazily against my chest. We sit in the quiet for a long time, but I can only stand being this close to her for so long.

"Okay, you need to take a shower."

She jerks her head up and gives me a death glare. "That's rude."

I close my eyes and pinch the bridge of my nose. "I'm sorry. I just can't sit here and smell you like this anymore. You're too enticing."

Her eyes dip with guilt, so I smack her on the butt playfully and she squeals.

"Come on. Let's get ready for bed."

We get up from the couch, but she pauses before reaching the stairs. Her voice is quiet when she says, "I don't want to sleep in my room."

So we head upstairs to my bedroom, and after we're settled, I fall asleep to the idea of calling it ours.

PART FOUR:
New Moon

Chapter Thirty

RAEGAN

Going back to the bookstore on Monday morning feels like going back to school after being out for a long break. Typically, I would be excited to see my friends and catch up with various members of town, but I find myself wishing I could stay at home with Jamie in the little bubble we've made.

Exploring the way our bodies work together and crave one another has been equally fascinating and exhilarating. I've found it's very easy to lose myself memorizing the lines of every muscle and tracing every inch of his skin. Besides the occasional need for food and water, I think I'd be perfectly fine never leaving the bed.

The mate bond is just like Jamie described: being near him empowers me to do things I've never done before, want things I've never wanted. He's like a drug, and no temptation on earth could lure me away from him. It's almost dizzying, the way he affects my senses. Everything looks brighter, tastes sweeter, and—

And now Ethan is staring at me like I snorted a line of

sugar.

"Good morning," he greets me warily.

"Good morning, Ethan! How are you this gorgeous fall morning?"

I've always been pleasant first thing in the morning, but I must have turned it up a notch too high based on the way he's raising his brow at me.

Oh, no. Do I have a post-orgasm glow? Is it that obvious?

"Fine," Ethan drones. "I take it your cheery attitude means you're ready to get back to work?" He suggests this with an expectant tone, and with sudden guilt, I realize my week-long absence meant leaving Ethan alone to open and close the store himself. Bound and Buried employs a handful of part-time workers, but typically Ethan and I split the managerial duties. It's not like me to be so inconsiderate, but this past week truly has thrown me off my game.

"Absolutely," I tell him. "Where do you want me to start?"

He points absentmindedly to a plastic bin sitting in front of the register labeled FALL DECOR. "Might as well start with the window display."

My mood skyrockets at the prospect of spending the morning decorating the three pane window looking out onto Main Street. It's been one of my favorite parts of the job. I would've thought the task would be finished by now, most likely handed off to one of the part-time employees, because the rest of town was decorated for fall weeks ago.

I go to the back office and put away my bag and the cozy cardigan I've been wearing. When I come back out, I grab the plastic bin and carry it closer to the window. Then a thought occurs to me: *Did Ethan purposefully postpone decorating the window until I got back?*

Now *that* would be ridiculous. Ethan knows how much I love being in charge of the window display, but he's never been that considerate, nor has he ever been kind to me after needing time off. But he was the one who offered it to me.

Shrugging it off, I spend the next few hours filling the space with color like it's an empty canvas. I string paper sunflowers around the edge of the window sill, plaster cling-on pumpkins to the glass, and line the bottom of the sill with straw. Then I take my time creating pretty stacks of Halloween-themed books that line the bottom of the windows. I tie a few together with twine and stick them in baskets with fake sunflowers. With a few extra pumpkins sprinkled here and there, I'm pretty sure my task is complete, so I go outside to take a look.

The display is perfect. The colors and textures just scream fall, and at night, the added touch of fairy lights will make it even better.

I'm admiring my work when I hear my name being called by a familiar voice. I turn to see Jo walking briskly down the street holding a cup of coffee in each hand, holding one out to me when she approaches.

"I had to come into town for dog food and thought I'd stop by," she says. "The window looks great!"

"Thanks!" I'm beaming at the combination of admiring my creativity and seeing Joanna again so soon.

Getting to talk with Jo this weekend about my conflicting feelings for Jamie was an outlet I hadn't known I needed, and seeing her again only reminds me how happy I am that she reached out in the first place.

Jo quirks a brow at me, just like Ethan did before. "What's got you so happy this morning?"

I shrug my shoulders and feign nonchalance. "I'm having a good day."

She glances at her watch. "It's only ten A.M."

"Okay," I concede, "it's been a good two hours."

Jo's eyes light up like a Christmas tree, and she clamps her hand dramatically over her mouth, suppressing a squeal.

I know exactly what she thinks she's figured out, so very calmly, I try to defuse the situation without drawing attention.

What is it about the front of this store that makes people want to cause a spectacle?

"It's not what you think," I tell her hastily.

She points directly at my lying face. "You decided to take a test drive, didn't you?"

I draw up short, because yes, I most definitely did. But I don't want the rest of Main Street to know that.

"Would you get over here?" I usher her into the store where the remnants of my decorating spree are strewn around the window and on the floor. Ethan is standing at the front counter and staring at me blankly, so I take that as a hint that I need to clean up before more customers arrive.

"Here," I say, handing Jo a wad of my paper scraps, "help me with this and I'll tell you everything."

She does so without question, practically bouncing on the balls of her feet while we clean up the rest of my mess. We toss everything back into the original bin and I close the lid. Nodding to the back of the store, I tell Jo that I'll be right back.

I put the bin in its proper place, and when I come back out to the floor, I tell Ethan I'm going to take a short break, and he miraculously doesn't argue. He just nods curtly and continues whatever he is doing.

Odd. Maybe he is trying to be kind to me today.

Jo and I sit on a bench outside tucked between the bookstore and Claudia's bakery. She hands me back my cup of coffee that I forgot about, and I take it happily. Taking a sip, I realize it's a pumpkin spice latte, but the cup says it's from Double Double.

"What is this? Jamie doesn't sell anything with pumpkin spice."

Jo smiles at me knowingly. "He does now."

"What made him change his mind?"

She pretends to think really hard, rubbing her chin and squinting her eyes. "Let's see. Perhaps it has to do with what you were about to tell me earlier. You know, about you deciding to have a little fun together."

She nudges me in the side playfully, and I cave. "Okay. Yes. We moved to second base."

"Second base?" she grimaces. "You're gonna have to be more specific. I don't play sports."

Jo waits with bated breath as I take a sip of my latte and mutter the words. "He used his mouth this time."

"Girl, use your words."

Though I've found my courage when I'm alone with Jamie, it's still awkward for me to talk about these things openly for some reason. I've never felt confident when it comes to sex.

I try again. "He went down on me. You know, he performed oral."

Joanna raises an eyebrow. "You know that's third base, right? But forget about that, how was it?"

Part of me wants to keep the intimate details of what's happened between me and Jamie to myself, but I don't see any harm in sharing the basic overview.

"It was...amazing." I sigh like a lovestruck schoolgirl, and I realize just how smitten I really am. "I was a little nervous at first, but I just went with my gut like you said, and it wasn't awkward or bland at all. I don't think I've ever connected to someone like that sexually before. And we haven't even had sex yet."

Jo gasps in mock horror. "You didn't take him for a full test drive?"

"Stop," I tease. "I tested several of the features, and I'm definitely interested."

"Well, well, well. Look at you. I have to say, as soon as I saw you up close, I could see a glow about you."

"Ugh, I knew it," I groan. "Everyone can tell, can't they?"

She hums thoughtfully. "Not always, but with you it's pretty obvious."

I lean my head back against the brick wall of the building and fake a cry.

"Don't worry," Jo says, perfunctorily patting my leg. "Maybe with the festival coming up, everyone will be so busy they won't notice two of Shadow Hills' resident B.F.F.s are finally fucking."

"Jo!"

She stands up abruptly and begins walking backwards away from the bench. "Gotta go get that dog food," she redirects the conversation. "Keep me posted on which bases you hit next."

She swings an imaginary bat then turns around and heads across the street, leaving me speechless and considering texting Jamie to ask what time he takes lunch.

Chapter Thirty-One

JAMIE

Things between Raegan and I have settled into a comfortable routine of waking up in the same bed, going to work separately, sometimes sharing our lunch breaks, then meeting back at home only to spend the rest of the evening learning all the possible ways I can make her cum, only to secretly relieve myself in the shower later. It's been exhilarating, and a little bit exhausting, given I tend to stay up way too late doing that last part.

Raegan surprises me every day with how open she's become towards her own sexuality. For someone who used to be timid and shy about anything sexual, she has truly blossomed into a confident and curious version of herself. I love seeing the wildness in her eyes when she decides to make the first move.

Earlier this week, she caught me completely off guard by coming into Double Double one mid-afternoon and asking for something not on the menu. She looked me right in the eye, unwavering, and ordered the three bean soup. I had no clue what she was referring to, because we do not offer soup, have never offered soup, but the longer those knowing eyes bore into me, I eventually put it together.

We made a show of me needing to get the ingredients from the back and her offering her assistance, though I'm pretty confident Casey knew exactly what we were doing. They just shook their head and took over the register while Raegan and I slipped to my office.

I barely had the door closed before she was sitting on my desk, shucking off her jeans. It wasn't until after I stroked her to climax twice, making sure she saw stars both times, that I figured out what her secret order meant.

"Three bean soup," I guffawed. "You ordered a vanilla soy latte."

Raegan smirked at me with a satisfied grin and kissed me fiercely. "Took you a minute."

Thinking back on our clandestine encounters, it occurs to me that I've never been happier in my life. Things just feel right, and for once, I don't dread the next lunar cycle. Though I know shifting is something I'll never be able to completely avoid, it feels a little less daunting knowing Raegan will be by my side. More than that, the thought of shifting doesn't bother me as much.

Being a werewolf feels like such a separate part of who I am, having kept that identity secret for so long, but Raegan has embraced it so boldly, I'm starting to consider whether or not the secret was worth it.

What would be so bad about just accepting what I am with grace? It's not like I'll ever be able to escape it. I've wasted so much time resenting the control the moon has over me, stuck in a ritualistic routine of bowing to its will every damn lunar cycle, but what if I'd spent that time at peace instead? I could have had this sacred time with Raegan so much sooner. If only I'd embraced my inner wolf from the beginning, perhaps the mating bond would have manifested the moment we met.

As I start setting up the Double Double booth for Founders Day on Tuesday morning, I decide to officially let go of all the fear and doubt I've harbored towards being a werewolf. I've spent so long being afraid of the moon and the control it holds over me, but each time I lose myself in a pair of lips I now know better than my own, I no longer need to be afraid. Because Raegan is my new moon, and I will follow her anywhere.

The only issue is how to come out to the town. Technically, by not declaring myself a paranormal when I first moved to Shadow Hills, I've been breaking the law for the past sixteen years. I'll have to plan a sitdown with Mayor Musthaven and explain my situation. Hopefully, given he's a paranormal himself and understands the complexities of being such, he'll give me a break. I decide I'll wait until after the festival. No need to distract him with my poor decisions while he's got so much on his plate.

Pushing that dilemma out of my mind for future me to solve, I focus on the activity around me. If anyone thought the center of town couldn't get any more decked out for fall, they'd be wrong. On top of the pumpkins, stacks of hay, and colorful florals already lining the windows and doors of every business, those same decorations now flood the sidewalks and extend onto the cobblestones of Main Street.

In front of each storefront sits wooden booths filled with wares specific to each business. Everyone is given free reign to customize and decorate the space to their liking. I've never put too much thought into the look of our booth, but this year I feel inspired. Maybe it's just my good mood translating over to the fall spirit, but I decide to line the top of our sign with fairy lights and a garland of orange leaves.

I also decided to add a pumpkin spice latte to our menu last week. Don't get me wrong, it's just a simple latte. No extra foam or fancy syrups. Just your basic pumpkin flavor with nutmeg and cinnamon. Another instance of my recent good mood influencing me to give the people what they want. I even added skulls to the shelves inside the coffee shop, but only for this weekend.

The festival starts at noon, so there's another hour before the Founding Day festivities officially start. I decide to head over to the Bound and Buried booth to see what Raegan has adorned the space with this year.

It turns out I'm not the only one in good spirits. Everyone in town is high on the excitement of their favorite time of year. I pass Kiki's Cafe where there's a makeshift bowling lane set up with hay bales, the ball being a small, perfectly round pumpkin. I wave at Kiki and Kendra behind their L-shaped booth where they're spooning out creamy tomato soup into styrofoam bowls. Kiki is wearing a bright orange sweatshirt with a jack-o-lantern face on the front. Kendra, on the other hand, has taken a more spooky approach to her outfit. Her face is painted white and her eyes are blacked out with dark makeup that runs down her cheeks. She's wearing an off-white victorian era dress that's torn in random places, eyelet lace draping lazily from the seams. She looks just like the image of a banshee from human folklore, no doubt her intention, and it's terrifying. I feel for any kids who cross her path.

I walk around a large seating area with tables for people to sit and eat their food and a cluster of apple bobbing bushels for kids, then cut across the courtyard in front of City Hall that's been cleared for a bonfire, fallen leaves crunching beneath my boots. Dodging strategically placed logs and blankets, I turn the corner and find Raegan's booth in front of the firehouse.

Instead of a covered wooden booth like the others, Bound and Buried has two long tables lined along the sidewalk. Both are draped with orange tablecloths and filled with stacks of books, covers facing up, as well as bookmarks, notepads and pens, stickers, and a handful of custom made book sleeves (Raegan owning one being the only reason I know what they're called). On either end of the tables are rolling carts filled with more books, but these are labeled with a little wooden plaque that reads SIGNED BY THE AUTHOR.

I'm about to call Reagan's name when I'm stopped cold by a sudden chill wracking my body. Mayor Musthaven then appears in front of me, having floated through me from behind.

"Sorry about that, Mr. Trent," he apologizes jovially.

"Mayor." I'm still trying to rub the feeling back into my arms since my long sleeve henley is doing nothing to warm me right now. "How's it going?"

"Oh you know," he drawls. "Looking forward to another successful Founding Day!" Then his expression dampens. "On the other hand, I was hoping to run into you."

Now I'm feeling chilled for a different reason. What purpose could the mayor possibly have to seek me out? "Why is that?" I ask cautiously.

"It's about that fellow who assaulted your friend, Miss Baker. I found out this morning from Sheriff Simmons that he was released on bail yesterday."

My inner wolf tilts its head. "He's out of jail?"

"Unfortunately," Mayor Musthaven bumbles, stroking his walrus mustache, "He must know someone with a decent amount of cash, because his bail was set pretty high, given the charges. But there's nothing to do now that it's paid. His court date isn't for several weeks, but he's free to be at home until then."

I've never been more grateful that Raegan finally moved in with me. There's no way in hell I'd want her living in the same building with that guy, especially now that he's got a grudge.

Patrick is probably furious at me, and Aidan, for making a fool out of him in front of the town, but over my dead body will I let him get any sort of revenge.

"Does the sheriff have extra patrols for the festival? They need to know there's a criminal on the loose with a motive to hurt someone." *Again.*

"They know, son. But you know the force doesn't have that kind of man power. And Twitty's about as threatening as a squirrel." He moves to place a hand on my shoulder for reassurance, but then thinks better of it when I grimace. "Don't worry. With this many people around, I doubt he'll try anything again."

It's more likely Patrick will take advantage of the large crowd and use it as the perfect distraction. But maybe the mayor is right. One: Twitty Simmons is a worthless sheriff, and two: everyone in Shadow Hills is going to be out and about on the streets today, which means dozens of sets of eyes to keep watch. All I have to do is spread the word, then I'll have the entire town helping me look out for Raegan's safety.

"Between you and me, can we keep this to ourselves?" I ask. "I'll tell her about it at a better time."

He looks to where Raegan and her coworkers are filling baskets with bookmarks and prints with quotes. "I understand," he agrees. "Wouldn't want to ruin a good day."

I give the mayor a nod and head straight for the bookstore's booth. It might be selfish, but I don't want Raegan catching wind of the news. Knowing Patrick is out of jail will only cause her unnecessary stress.

I surprise her by appearing at the end of the table when she turns around.

"Jamie!" Her smile is so big and so genuine, I decide it's the only ego boost I'll ever need. Knowing someone is *that* happy to see me, I have no reason to be sad ever again.

"Did you have this many books out last year?" I ask, picking up a random one and reading the title. "*Loving the Lochness Monster*." I immediately put it back. "Hard pass."

"Yes, we did," she answers, "and don't judge the monster romance."

"No judgment here." I wink. "Every monster deserves love."

Her expression turns serious, and she lightly strokes my forearm. "You're not a monster, Jamie."

Thanks to her, I'm starting to believe that.

I move closer, the invisible string between us pulling taut. I want to kiss her, but I'm not sure if she's ready for such a public display of affection. Instead, I squeeze her hip lightly beneath her cardigan. It's covered in patches of pumpkins and coffee mugs. Either she and Kiki coordinated, or I didn't get the ugly sweater memo. I thought wearing a flannel was festive.

"Come by my booth around noon and we'll walk around together," I suggest.

She smiles. "Alright."

I give her a wink as I walk away, and I swear I see her swoon a little. As I make my way back through the winding maze of tables and booths, I start spreading the word to keep watch for Patrick. Kiki and Kendra agree like it's their life mission, and I make sure to text Aidan, too. Hopefully, with enough people watching like hawks, there will be no surprises today.

Chapter Thirty-Two

RAEGAN

The warm touch of Jamie's hand on my hip lingers as I watch him disappear around the corner. Jamie's always been physically affectionate, but his touch has transformed into something more possessive. But not in a scary way—not like Patrick. Jamie claims me as his without showing force. He's a gentle summer breeze against my winter skin reminding me, and all others, he's there.

As the days have passed, I find myself wanting to accept the mate bond more and more. Constantly daydreaming about the ways he would claim me, both physically and emotionally, make me forget what I'm doing and lose track of time. The past week has felt like a dream itself. Each time we fall asleep tangled in one another, I find it a little easier to believe this could work, and maybe, this is what Jamie and I were meant to be all along.

The morning passes quickly thanks to the constant flux and flow of traffic in front of the booth. With most of the members of town manning their own stations, the visiting crowd of people is mostly made up of tourists. It's an interesting dynamic, the relationship between Shadow Hills and outside humans. The paranormals here were given no other choice but to leave the city, though giving them their own town to live freely was made to look like an offer of kindness. Truthfully, most humans might not want to live among paranormals, but they certainly have no problem flocking to see them every Halloween like a spectacle.

I used to think the only reason the town has embraced the tradition of the festival is because of the money it brings in, but residents here actually enjoy dressing up and poking fun at themselves. It's like an inside joke. They give humans what they want to see, and at the end of the day, they get to keep their real lives to themselves.

As for me, I happily greet every person who comes up to the booth, regardless of who they are. Because despite prejudices, I believe books can bring anyone together. I direct kids to coloring books and Choose Your Own Adventure stories, while pushing the mysteries and spooky romances to the parents. I even take time to say hello to a few of the coven members who stop by looking for books on earth magic. My mother isn't with them. Secretly, despite our tense conversation on the phone weeks ago, I wish she would have taken the time to check in with her only daughter.

The hours fly by, and soon it's time for my coworkers to take their breaks. I man the booth alone for the next fifteen minutes, and I've fallen into such a steady rhythm that I don't immediately register the next person in line. The man has a five o'clock shadow, and his shoulders are slumped, so he easily blends into the mass of people surrounding the table, but when I look up and see his cold gray eyes, my heart stops.

I don't recognize this stranger, but something about him is familiar. I try to place him as I give him a once over, deciding he's too old to be one of the boys I used to babysit. His hood is pulled over his head and his hand is shoved into his jacket pocket. I see the shape of something bulky protruding through the inner fabric. It's pointed directly at my stomach. Panicking, I freeze, assuming he has a gun.

Dozens of questions race across my mind. There's never been a reported shooting in Shadow Hills' history, so why would this man come here? And why is he aiming that weapon at me? More concerning than that is my uncertainty of whether or not he'll use that weapon in a crowd of people. Someone could get killed, but my gut tells me I'm his sole target.

My first thought is to duck under the table and hide, but I know that's not a smart option. I have to get him away from other people, especially the kids, and though my fear is threatening to swallow me whole right now, I take a deep breath and force my body to move.

I slowly inch around the table and away from the line that's formed, smiling reassuringly at the customers still browsing and telling them I'll be right back. I make sure to distance myself from the kids as much as possible before making my way from the sidewalk to the street, giving the table a wide berth. All the while, the man keeps his eyes on me.

He doesn't have to say a word, knowing the threat of him being there is enough to scare me into submission. He jerks his head to the right, aiming for me to follow his direction and move to somewhere secluded. I assume he means to get me in the side alley alone, but that is absolutely not going to happen. I'm not going to make the same mistake with this man that I did with Patrick.

Instead, I push further into the crowd. I know it's not the smartest thing to do, by hiding among strangers I put everyone around me at risk, but I am counting on the man's desire to not be noticed. He has to know if he draws attention to himself, the gig is up. It's why he's keeping his head low, making sure no one sees his face.

I try to keep enough distance between us so he can't sneak up on me. He's definitely here for me, but I can't pinpoint his plan. Will he try to get me into a car and steal me away somewhere? Or does he just want to kill me and be done with it?

I try to search my memory for any trace of his face as I continue to walk as calmly as possible down the street, sweat running down my back and hands shaking. I'm aiming for the Double Double booth. One look at me and Jamie will know something is wrong. But I don't want to make another scene like before.

I still don't know how this man knows me. Was I rude to him at the bookstore one day? Did I cut him off in traffic? A thousand possibilities flood my brain before I reach the seating area beside the Kiki's Cafe food stand. Jamie and the rest of the Double Double team are on the other side handing out lattes and fancy hot chocolate. There are about four people separating the man from me now as I try to catch Jamie's eye.

I hope with my entire being that the pull between us can somehow let him know when I'm in trouble. Jamie's form appears sporadically in the distance as people pass in front of where I'm standing, so I focus all of my attention on him.

Then, as if he's heard me call his name, he looks up.

Chapter Thirty-Three

JAMIE

I feel a pull in my gut, like the universe is nudging me to get my attention, and I'm compelled to glance out into the crowd. My eyes fall directly onto Raegan. She's standing stark still in the seating area next to Kiki's while everyone else moves around her. She's as pale as a ghost, and my heart drops at the clear fear on her face.

I'm racing to her before my brain has even registered my legs are moving. I have to get to her. I have to make sure she's okay. Nothing is more important right now. But as I push through the crowd of visitors dressed in fall hues, I detect a dark spot among the colors.

A man in a black zip up hoodie is standing a few feet behind Raegan. His eyes are trained on her like a predator locking in on their prey. I can't get a clear view of the man's face, but all my senses tell me it's Patrick. Though I made sure to prep my closest friends for his possible return, I hadn't truly believed he would show up.

I should have known a man like Patrick would be relentless in his quest for revenge. Men like Patrick don't just brush off an insult to their pride by getting even. Men like Patrick want to win, and in his eyes, that means having Raegan. I guarantee he's currently sorting through all the ways he can whisk her away without anyone being the wiser, but I'll be dead before that happens.

I'm nearly close enough to reach out and pull Raegan to my side when I see Kendra approaching him. She must have spotted him about the same time I spotted Raegan, but what in the world does she think she's doing? I didn't want the sisters putting themselves in harm's way. I only told them to keep an eye out for anyone suspicious. Little did I know Kendra would be brave enough to confront Patrick directly.

I manage to reach Raegan and protectively wrap my arms around her just as Kendra stares down Patrick with solid black eyes, exaggerated by the dramatic makeup. I've never seen them like that before, but looking at them makes me feel like I'm being sucked into an endless pit of doom. This is not the kind-hearted banshee I know and love. This is a myth from storybooks, come to life.

She starts to open her mouth, and Raegan and I hastily try to cover our ears, but before Kendra can release her ear-splitting cry, she's shoved backward. Others around us gasp as she falls clumsily to the sidewalk, nearly hitting her head on the cobblestones if not for a cluster of pumpkins breaking the impact.

My wolf threatens to break the surface as Raegan clings to my body. *Where the hell is that good-for-nothing sheriff?*

But then Aidan appears, having heard the commotion, and pops a pair of fake vampire teeth from his mouth, shoving them in his pocket before going to Kendra's side. Then Kiki is there, helping her sister to her feet.

I was angry before, but now I'm outright enraged.

This mother fucker has got the go.

It's then that I fully see the man's face, and I realize I had all my fear staked on the wrong guy. It's not Patrick standing in front of me, but Banks—the wolf Rhett warned me might try to exile me from the pack and steal Raegan.

Before I can fully process this realization, Banks pulls a knife from his pockets and lashes out. I try to yank Raegan out of his reach, but I'm not fast enough, and the blade slices messily through her sweater and the back of her forearm. Her scream of pain breaks through any shred of self control I still hold onto.

This mother fucker has to die.

One minute, I'm shoving Raegan behind me just as Aidan sweeps her away, and the next, I'm lunging for Banks' throat.

Chapter Thirty-Four

RAEGAN

At first, I'm not sure what just happened.

I felt a quick sting of pain on my forearm, but I didn't see where it came from. I assume it had to be from the guy's weapon he'd been hiding, but I was moved out of the way so quickly, I didn't get a chance to see.

Only a second ago I was tucked away safely in Jamie's arms, but now I'm surrounded by Aidan's cool touch. He's pulling me backward into the crowd and away from the space that's opened up around Jamie and the assailant. I watch in what feels like slow motion as Jamie's back muscles tense and grow in front of my eyes.

His flannel rips in half and hangs from his arms in shreds. His back hunches as his body curls inward, all while muscles stretch and lengthen. His knees bend backward. His neck thickens. And in a matter of seconds, a wolf replaces a full grown man.

Seeing Jamie shift is shocking—scary even—but seeing the menace in his eyes as a wolf is more terrifying than anything I've ever seen before.

The man stands unflinching as Jamie pounces, even when Jamie's teeth come within inches of his face. He just steps out of the way as if he's a superhero dodging a bullet. They both move with such agile speed.

The crowd lets out a collective scream, and people start running in different directions. I don't know which way is what, but Aidan manages to direct us to the sidewalk and out of the chaos. The tourists have all scattered, but everyone else is staring open-mouthed at the sight of a fully shifted wolf. Like me, I don't think most of Shadow Hills' residents have seen the werewolves in their wolf forms, so this must be a huge shock.

Jamie then catches the man by his pant leg forcing him to the ground. I fear how far he is willing to go now that he's in the body of a predator. He has every reason to mutilate this stranger beyond recognition for what he's done, but Jamie's attacks feel personal. Like he knows him.

I whirl around to face Aidan. "Do you know who that is?"

He doesn't answer. Right now he's busy ripping off the bottom half of his button up. He pulls my injured arm out of my sweater and I wince. Blood trickles down to my fingers as he tightens the scrap of material around the gash. It's starting to pulse with pain. When Aidan is done, he scans the crowd as if looking for someone.

I decide to discard my sweater, now torn and stained with blood anyway, leaving my simple white baby tee underneath. "Who is that?" I demand, this time more urgently.

Aidan's jaw clenches. "I don't know. But he smells like a wolf." His words are clipped like it's taking all of his concentration to speak. My blood must be getting to him. Instinctively, I take a step back, but he grabs my uninjured arm.

"Stay with me," he says firmly. "I'm fine."

I'm not entirely sure he's telling the truth, but I trust him enough to look back to the scene before us just as the man is getting back to his feet. Jamie's attention isn't where it's supposed to be. He's looking at me, probably checking to make sure I'm alright.

The man takes advantage of Jamie's distraction. "Look at you," he taunts, "shifting into the thing you hate only when it serves you."

Is this man another werewolf? If so, why are they infighting? He's clearly confident, steady in whatever his reasoning is, but unless he plans to shift himself, he should know better than to bait a massive werewolf while in his human form.

Jamie snarls, teeth bared.

"Don't you wanna know why I finally decided to make my move?" the man continues. Jamie simply paces back and forth, biding his time.

Just attack him! I scream internally. But then I think better of it. No one else knows the man is a werewolf. If Jamie attacks a man who looks human in front of the entire town, he could face major repercussions. That has to be why he's waiting for the right moment.

"My dear cousin called saying he's in jail and needed help, so I bailed him out."

My stomach drops. *Is he talking about Patrick?*

"He's really pissed at you," the man continues. "He wanted to come to the festival himself—look you in the eye—but I told him I'd have his back." He leers, a wicked grin cutting across his face. "All the more reason to finally put you in your place."

Jamie looks like he's ready to shred this man to ribbons and rip out his sternum, but I can't let him make that mistake. Not unless the other werewolf shifts.

I fight against Aidan's hold around my upper arm and attempt to run out there. Maybe Jamie will recognize me and back off, not wanting to cause me harm. But Aidan's grip is like a statue, unwavering and solid.

"Why don't you do something?" I yell. *Why can't you just step in and diffuse the situation like last time?*

Aidan looks from me to Jamie and back again. He knows he should stop his friend from doing something he can't take back, yet he continues to stand here.

"Aidan!"

He only presses his lips together and glances around uneasily, then he grimaces and squeezes his eyes shut. "I can't. Seeing me will only make it worse."

"Why?" I'm feeling frenzied. I can't help thinking we're only moments from something really terrible happening, and it's going to be all my fault.

"Because," Aidan barks, and I flinch, "I'm a vampire, Raegan. My smell will just distract him. It doesn't matter that we're friends. While he's fully shifted, his senses only tell him there's another predator in his territory, and he'll have to focus on me instead."

I don't want it to, but his explanation makes sense.

Suddenly, Aidan's eyes lock onto something in the distance. Some*one*.

"Stop!"

I scan the crowd wildly trying to find the source of the booming voice. Then I see him. Rhett is running toward us from the other end of the street. He's not wearing the leather jacket this time, just a plain black T-shirt and jeans. His heavy boots pound against the cobblestones as he races to the scene, long red hair flying behind him.

My initial reaction is to groan at the sight of another werewolf, but then I remember he's the alpha. They'll have to listen to him.

"Banks," Rhett bellows the name, coming to a halt directly behind where the other werewolf is standing. "Stop this, *now*."

The alpha's voice is steady and calm, but his tone is direct, leaving no room for question. Both Jamie and the other man—Banks—seem to have a physical reaction to Rhett's words. Jamie tucks his head low while Banks jerks like a shiver just wracked his spine.

"This is over," Rhett commands. "Both of you, go back to the camp. I'll meet you there."

Jamie looks away from his alpha, and I think he might attempt to defy him, but then I realize he's looking for me. I move to the front of the crowd and hold Jamie's stare. I nod my head, letting him know I'm okay. Then he's bounding past the stunned spectators and heading straight for the woods outside of town. I let out the breath I didn't realize I was holding.

"Raegan." I'm startled by my name being called, but it's Rhett. "Come with me."

Chapter Thirty-Five

RAEGAN

Several hours pass while I anxiously walk circles in the grass, waiting for Jamie to come out and tell me everything's alright. After Rhett insisted I come with him, I followed him to a rusted yellow Jeep, and we rode in silence to the pack's property.

When we got to camp, Paloma made it a priority to properly clean and cover my wound. The cut from Banks' knife wasn't as deep as I thought it would be, so I was able to avoid stitches. It still hurts, so she gave me an aspirin to help fight infection and pain, making it feel a little better.

But as I pace back and forth in front of their house, my brain spits out all the ways Jamie might get out of facing repercussions for his actions. Surely Sheriff Simmons wouldn't want to get involved in werewolf affairs, and Rhett wouldn't punish Jamie for protecting me. He did what he thought was necessary at that moment.

But then I wonder what the rest of town will say.

Jamie put people in danger just as much as Banks by shifting in front of everyone. There's a reason why he goes off to the woods alone every full moon. Though I now know for certain the mate bond prevents Jamie from hurting me in his wolf form, I can't say the same about anyone else. Even Aidan said Jamie wouldn't remember that he's a friend.

I'm so wired I feel like I could power an entire city. I haven't been able to sit down since arriving at the campground.

Jo called when she heard about what happened. She wasn't at the festival, but by the time I talked to her, she already had the details from those who were. I tried to convince her I was okay, but I've learned by now those efforts are usually fruitless. She showed up ten minutes later, demanding to be let in the front gate. I think she actually scared Tyler.

Aidan is here too, but apparently he wasn't scary enough to be let onto the property. It seems the vampire and werewolf beef really does run deep.

"Don't they have, like, a mate clause in the werewolf handbook?" Joanna asks, twirling her hair nervously.

It sounds crazy, but I would love for there to be a handbook with some fucking rules in it for once.

But I don't say anything. So Jo goes for something else. "Can you stop doing that? You're making me a little dizzy."

When she got here, I had to give her a rough recap of everything that's happened over the past two weeks, and I'm grateful she's taken this whole werewolf situation so well, but her calmness is starting to push my buttons. "What else am I supposed to do?"

Her response is cut off when the door to the building finally opens. Rhett steps out onto the porch and gives me a reassuring nod. I sink to the ground in relief, and my body crashes. I've been so tense waiting for news it feels like I've been hit by a truck now that I can finally relax.

Jamie comes out next. He's wearing a black T-shirt just like Rhett's and a pair of plaid pajama pants, having lost his clothes to the shift. He appears stricken with guilt as he stares at his own feet.

Rhett walks straight over to me and crouches down, placing a steady hand on my back. "He's not in trouble."

I look up dazed. "What?"

Rhett smirks knowingly. "Mayor Musthaven and Sheriff Simmons claim to have been too caught up in a pumpkin bowling match to have seen what happened." Though I'm grateful, I know very well that's a lie, and they know it too. "But after we left, they managed to convince the tourists it was all part of a planned Halloween skit."

No doubt there was likely some witchcraft involved in the convincing. I'll have to ask the coven about that.

I frown and blink rapidly. "But what about Banks?"

Rhett doesn't miss a beat. "He threatened a fellow pack member's mate. He'll be facing his own consequences."

"But we're not..."

Jamie steps up then and adds, "He might have forgotten to mention we haven't sealed that bond yet."

I feel heat rush to my cheeks, but Rhett doesn't appear bothered by knowing the intimate details of mine and Jamie's relationship. Instead, he gives me a reassuring grin and helps me to my feet.

"Maybe you can fix that," he suggests to Jamie, followed by a laugh from Jo that she tries to disguise as a cough.

And now my entire body is on fire.

Jamie gives him a pinched expression and tugs at his shirt. It's a little too tight, but it clings to his muscles in all the right ways. "I appreciate your help," he tells his uncle. "I really do. But we've got it from here."

Rhett heads back up the stairs of the camper and salutes. "Whatever you say."

Jamie looks to me. "Can we go home now?"

"Yes, please." I take a step toward Jamie's outstretched arms. As I rest my head against his chest, feeling the subtle beat of his heart in my ear, I feel more at home than I ever have.

"Come on," Joanna says, "I'll drop you off."

Aidan is standing like a creepy statue as we reach the front gate. Jamie and I are used to his lack of need to breathe, but he seems to have taken Joanna by surprise, because she startles.

"Who the hell is that?"

Aidan frowns. "Who are you?"

"I'm Joanna Shepherd: friend and bodyguard. And you," she points to Aidan's stiff frame, "do not look like a werewolf."

Jamie stifles a laugh and I hide my face in his side.

Aidan crosses his arms and narrows his eyes, taking in the feisty human mouthing off to him. "Why do you say that?"

Joanna doesn't miss a beat. "Because you're, I dunno, pale?"

I burst out laughing, and she turns to give me a clueless expression. "What? He is!"

"I'm pale, Jo. What is that supposed to mean?"

She side-eyes Aidan who is still glaring at her. "You just have fair skin," she explains. "This guy looks like a vampire."

Aidan's face is vibrating with disgust.

I can tell he wants to say something smart, but Jamie coughs and clears his throat. "Joanna, meet my friend, Aidan. He's a vampire."

Her eyes go wide and her face flushes with embarrassment. I decide to relieve her of her suffering and leave Jamie's side to go to hers.

"He's not as scary as he looks," I reassure her. But she only grumbles to herself. "And he can walk home."

Aidan takes the hint and speeds off in the blink of an eye, leaving Jo even more stunned.

Jamie gets behind the wheel of Jo's SUV and drives us back to the condo. Throughout the ride, I think about how wild these past two weeks have been, but I can't say I regret anything. If not for all the scary moments, I wouldn't have a new best friend to lean on, and I wouldn't be so certain of how much I want to be with Jamie. Because while he's still my best friend, he's now so much more.

Jamie is the love of my life...and I want to be his mate.

Chapter Thirty-Six

JAMIE

When we finally get back to the condo, the two of us look like we've just fought a war. We're both mentally exhausted from what happened at the festival, and my body is tired from the shift. Raegan is probably ready to lock herself in her room to get away from me. I wouldn't blame her. The amount of stress I've caused her makes me feel like the worst friend ever. It certainly doesn't make me worthy of being her mate.

I think she's about to head upstairs, but she surprises me by stopping in the living room. When she turns to face me, her eyes are misty and brimmed with tears. I move to her instinctively, knowing this might be the last time she lets me get this close, but once I get closer, I see she's smiling.

She's not upset or scared. She looks...happy.

"Raegan?" I brush her hair away from her face. "Are those happy tears?"

Her voice is rich with emotion when she says, "I want to accept the mate bond."

I stutter. "Y-you, you w-what?"

She giggles and displays a wide grin. "I'm choosing forever with you Jamie Trent. I want to be your mate."

I straighten and fully focus my gaze on the fading marks on Raegan's throat. They've almost healed, yet all I can think about is how me being with her might add more.

"Are you sure that's what you want, Rae? Just look at yourself. You're literally battered and bruised, and it all started because of how I acted with Patrick."

"It all started because you thought I was a burglar and accidentally cut me with a kitchen knife," she corrects. But then her cheery demeanor fades, and I see the fear behind her smile. "I was really scared I was going to lose you," she admits quietly, as fresh tears stream down her face. "Just the thought of you being taken away from me, I couldn't bear it."

"Hey, I'm not going anywhere." I wipe the tears from her cheeks with my thumbs and kiss her softly. "I was scared too," I confess, still holding her close. "You being in any kind of danger makes me feel like my heart is outside my chest. I want to be able to protect you, but I don't want to smother you."

"Will me being your mate make it easier?" she asks in earnest.

I shake my head. "I don't know. This is all new to me. But it would at least let me feel more connected to you. I'd be able to feel when you're in pain."

Raegan lifts her chin. "Then that's what I want."

"You're sure?" I have to ask at least one more time.

"I am *one thousand percent* sure." She makes sure to use my own words, so I know she's serious.

I take her freshly bandaged arm in my hands. Once again, I'm grateful for Aidan's quick thinking, and even more unsure of how I'll ever repay him for his kindness. Vampires and werewolves aren't known to be friendly, but Aidan has gone out of his way to save Raegan twice now.

"Looks like we've come full circle," I murmur softly as I press her hand against my chest. "Let's go to bed."

We take our time climbing the stairs, all the while holding tight to one another with clasped fingers. She might have confirmed her willingness to accept the bond, but this thing between us still feels too good to be true. I don't think I'll be one hundred percent confident until I'm locked inside her. I just hope she doesn't freak out over what's about to happen.

If I warn her about knotting ahead of time, I worry she won't be able to enjoy the sex. Her mind will be focused on what's coming next throughout the entire process, and I'd hate for our first time to be ruined by her anxious thoughts. But I don't want to lie to her either. Truthfully, I don't know exactly what's going to happen. Knotting only happens between mates, so I'm not sure how to warn of something I don't even know how to describe.

As we enter my bedroom—the one that, after tonight, will officially be ours—I decide the way to do this is to be completely honest and guide her through it.

We're sweaty and still frazzled by the day's events, but as I watch her remove her shirt after stopping at the foot of the bed, I'm lost in the sight of how beautiful she is. Even nervous, hands shaking as she moves to strip off her pants next, she looks perfect. She's facing away from me, and I find myself leaning at the door frame admiring her petite frame and delicious curves, her pale skin illuminated in the moonlight coming through the bedroom window.

She turns to see me staring, and for a second, I think she's going to cover herself, embarrassed by me watching her for so long, but she doesn't. Instead, she walks confidently over to where I'm standing and fists the front of my shirt in her delicate fingers. I grab the back of my collar and pull the shirt over my head as she draws lines down my stomach. My muscles clench beneath her touch, and I can't believe I've managed to hold out this long.

"These too," she demands seductively, tugging lightly on the pair of pajama pants I borrowed from Rhett. Turns out I was wrong, he does own plaid.

I slide out of them with one hand, along with my boxers, while keeping the other on Raegan's slender shoulder. I will never not be in awe of how soft she feels beneath my touch.

She looks at me fully for the first time, taking in everything I have on display for her. As she looks her fill, I'm a bit self-conscious. My cock is hard and swollen at the base, something she's probably never seen before, but she doesn't appear to be put off by it. Only curious.

I gently move her back to the bed, and she falls flat on her back with a small giggle, head sinking between the pillows. I adjust them so she's propped up. Her smile is unlike any drug, and the feeling of her smooth flesh beneath my touch elicits the most unique euphoria I will ever experience. She is my entire world, my moon and my sun. I want to revolve around her and just exist in her presence.

I take my time exploring the hills and valleys of her body. Raegan's skin raises as I trail my fingers up her legs. When I reach her hip, I lean down to plant an open-mouthed kiss on her stomach. She whimpers as I move up her torso and feel my way to her breasts. I take one nipple between my teeth and tug with delicate precision, and I hear little moans leave her mouth, making my head spin.

Raegan's hands are searching across the plane of my back, and as I move between her legs, her thighs fall to either side. My erection slides painfully against the inside of her soft thigh as I situate myself above her. I have to fight the urge to bear down and gain more friction.

I look at her face, hoping to see nothing but pure bliss, but she's biting her lip worriedly. I know she's enjoying this, but I can tell the difference between Raegan biting her lip seductively and Raegan stressing herself out for no reason. I was right about her being anxious about the mate bond, but I don't know how to stop it.

"Hold that thought," I say, getting up suddenly.

Her legs fall to the bed and she scowls. "What're you doing?"

I race from my bedroom buck naked and across the hall to hers. Cleetus is lying on his back in Raegan's new bed, snoring in sleepy bliss. I ignore him and go to her bookshelves, searching for the book she'd been listening to on her phone last week. Based on her confession, I know she keeps a physical copy of everything she listens to, but I actually let out a 'ah-ha!' when I recognize the cover.

Pulling it from the shelf, I hurry back to where Raegan is now sitting in my bed with a dumbfounded expression on her face. "What are you doing?"

I hand her the book and flick on the light beside the bed. "I wanna hear you read that spicy scene out loud while I feast on that pretty pussy of yours."

Raegan's blush floods her cheeks and extends to her neck, but I don't want her to overthink this. I want her to feel confident and sexy. I don't simply want her to tell me what she likes, I want her to learn new things about herself. Things she never knew she wanted before and only I can provide.

She takes the book from my hands and flips right to the specified chapter. The first page has been dog-eared.

"Raegan," I playfully scold her, "have you marked the page?

She looks up at me sheepishly. "I might have re-read it," she admits. "Twice."

"Welp, third time's the charm." I yank her carefully back

down onto the bed and she squeals. I make sure her head is properly supported by the pillows before laying on my stomach between her thighs, then wait patiently for her to start reading. "Go on then."

"Jamie, this is weird."

"No, it's not. Don't overthink it. Just read it as if you're reading it to yourself, only I'll be acting it out. It'll be a 4D experience."

I glance up to see she's giving me the most deadpan you're-an-idiot expression I've ever seen, and I can't help but laugh. But then she lets out a sigh and settles back into position.

She starts to read. "'*His tongue stroked languid lines along my folds*', ugh, gross. I don't like that word."

"Raegan."

"Okay, okay. '*I shuddered at the feel of him gliding through my wetness. His eyes peered up at me, starving, as if the taste of me was so good, he would never be able to fully satiate himself.*'"

I'm trying my hardest not to laugh, because I can hear the cringe in her tone, but when I finally press a kiss to her clit, her hips jerk slightly. "Keep going."

She obeys, reading through the next paragraph with more confidence as I start to press harder against her clit with my tongue. When I slide a finger inside her, her breath hitches between the words. I stroke slowly with my tongue while I start to pump in and out of her, eventually adding another finger. She's starting to fidget, and I know she wants to move faster, harder, so I pick up the pace with my fingers, slamming my knuckles against her opening as I suck on her delicate bundle of nerves.

She lets out a small cry, and I feel the book she's holding fall against the top of my head. She definitely isn't reading anymore, and by what I can tell, she isn't stressing anymore either.

I pound my fist into her slick heat, my fingers hitting the spot I know she wants. Her cry turns into a long and downright pornographic moan. Without looking, I reach above my head and toss the book to the floor, leaving room for me to find the curve of her breasts. I run my thumb over her hardened nipple just as I lift my head and switch my entire focus to the relentless thrusts of my hand. She's dripping around my fingers, and I'm moving so fast I almost slip out of rhythm a few times, but then I see her mouth fall open, signaling the start of her climb to climax.

My muscles are starting to cramp, but I don't let up. I follow through until she's writhing and crying out. When it's too much, she grabs my hand and pulls it away, so I stop, placing gentle kisses along her pelvis instead.

"Jamie."

"Yes."

"I-I can't feel my legs."

I chuckle. "Lemon, we're just getting started."

Chapter Thirty-Seven

RAEGAN

The muscles in my legs are spent. I feel used in the best possible way. But now I'm afraid I might have asked for too much. I've never enjoyed foreplay with other partners. Most guys just spend a few seconds down there thinking their goal is just for me to be wet enough to slide their dick in. Honestly, I haven't minded skipping to the home run. Getting it over quickly made sense when I didn't experience the same type of orgasm I could give myself.

But holy shit.

Jamie has coaxed more earth-shattering orgasms from me in the past two weeks than I've ever been able to accomplish with my vibrator, much less another man. I almost don't want to continue to the next part, because if he's able to destroy me with his dick the way he just did with his fingers, I might not survive it.

He looks velvety soft and delightfully hard. When he catches me staring, he grabs himself and tugs lightly, and I try to imagine what the precum dripping from his tip would taste like. I want to watch him lose all inhibitions from my touch just as he's managed to unwind me so easily. But I'm still unsure about the process of this mate bond.

I don't know much about werewolf anatomy, but Jamie's penis definitely does not look like any I've seen before. The base is slightly swollen and looks a little painful.

"Are you alright?"

He stills, and in a less confident tone says, "I'm okay. It's what I was trying to tell you about before. It only happens with werewolves when they mate."

"What happens?"

He strokes himself absentmindedly again, and I'm starting to think it might actually be uncomfortable for him.

"If I cum inside you," he explains, "the base will swell and lock me inside you." His eyes go wide when he registers the look of panic on my face. "But only for a few minutes," he promises. "Then it'll start to go down."

This is definitely not what I envisioned when he tried to explain all of this a few days ago. "Is that normal?"

"Yes. It's why I didn't want to have sex until you were ready. The process can be...intense."

A spark of jealousy strikes me. "Has it happened before?"

Jamie reaches for my cheek and pulls my forehead flush with him. "No, Rae. I've just been given an idea of what to expect. And I want to do the same for you."

I nod slowly, knowing he would never put me in a situation that made me uncomfortable. And he respects me too much to blindside me.

"Okay," I whisper, my lips grazing his.

He kisses me slowly, lingering as he sucks my bottom lip. His tongue explores mine, and I feel my core start to tingle again. I'm already sore from how hard Jamie fingered me, but I relished it. The forceful way he pounded into me coaxed me above and beyond the scope of pleasure I once knew into brand new territory. I want to break more barriers, but I'm not sure I can take a rough round of intercourse. But I don't want him to hold back.

Not without difficulty, he breaks our kiss and reaches over to the bedside table and pulls out a condom. I slide further down the sheets so my head is flat against the bed as he slips it on. Then Jamie positions himself above me as he starts to run his thumb along my seam again.

"Ready?"

His eyes are rich and warm, and I instantly relax. "Mmmhmm."

"You gotta say it, Raegan."

"I'm ready."

The tip of his cock presses against my entrance, and I have to fight the urge to just shove him inside me. I need that pressure again. But as I feel him slowly inch his way in, I think better of it. He's just as thick as he looked, and the further he goes, the further my inner walls stretch. My muscles are clenched too tight, but I can't stop the involuntary resistance.

"You gotta relax, baby." His low and steady voice whispers against my cheek as he hovers above me. "I've got you."

I nod, meeting his eyes. He works his way further in, and I can't stop the moan that leaves my mouth.

I start to unclench my muscles, and once he's fully sheathed I'm able to appreciate the fullness of him. I love it. It feels like my entire body is wrapped up in him. He slides an arm beneath my back while the other props himself up beside my head. He waits for me to be fully adjusted, then he starts moving.

We take it slow. A few short, easy pumps to get us going. Then, as I feel more comfortable, he speeds up. But never too fast. We find our rhythm, and slowly, I feel like I'm inching toward the peak of something, but I don't quite make it.

Having never experienced a vaginal orgasm, I'm not sure what to expect, but I know it should be more than this. "Something doesn't feel right."

He stops immediately and assesses my face, making sure I'm okay. "Does it hurt?"

"No, no," I assure him. "It's just not really doing anything for me."

He doesn't look offended, but he purses his lips as if he's trying to figure out a puzzle. Then his eyebrows lift, and I know he's got it.

"Flip over."

He sits back on his heels so I can roll over to my stomach. I rest my arms under my chin, waiting to see what he's planning, but then he hikes my hips into the air. A startled gasp is the only response I can give.

"Let me know if it's too much."

"I will."

When he enters me again, it's so much deeper than before. He's able to fully insert himself all the way to the hilt, and I feel the flat expanse of his core against my ass. He starts by simply rocking his hips and even this small movement is enough to trigger an involuntary moan from me. Whatever part of me he's touching in there feels like it's covered in a million nerve endings. It's almost too much, but he presses into me further, allowing the sensitivity to lessen.

His hand slides from my shoulder blade all the way down my back, sending shivers across my skin. He takes my hips in both hands, and I can sense he's looking at where we're connected, admiring how well we fit together.

Without warning, he pulls out and slams into me. I cry out. He pounds against my ass, sliding into my slick heat over and over, each time hitting that glorious spot inside me that only he can reach. I turn my face into the mattress and let out whatever ungodly noise necessary to get me through this. Because it's too much. It's not enough. And I'm pretty sure I've lost all sense of direction.

Blood rushes to my head and it feels like I'm floating. My stomach muscles start to not only flutter but actually clinch like I'm doing a set of sit-ups, and I know what I'm about to experience is unlike anything I've ever felt before.

As the first wave of my orgasm hits, my entire body contracts.

"Jamie! Oh god! Oh god! *Oh god!*"

He groans with his own pleasure. "You're taking me so good, baby."

"*Jamie!*"

"That's it. Good girl."

"Jamie?" This time there's a little bit of panic in my voice. "Are you getting bigger?"

He pulls me up so I'm flush to his chest and wraps his arms around me. "It's alright, Rae. You're doing great. Just keep relaxing for me, okay?"

After the third wave of relentless clenching and overwhelming pleasure, my body has no choice. I'm limp in Jamie's arms, but he's holding me tight enough to support my weight.

He groans again as he fills me. His cock swells to what feels like twice its size, but I remind myself it's just the base. We're officially locked together, and as Jamie continues to rotate his hips and utter the final notes of his orgasm against the back of my neck, I find I don't mind the sensation.

It's just slightly uncomfortable, but at the same time it feels...good.

We're both still on our knees as we come down from our high. I'm sore and over stimulated but the fullness of him locked inside me makes it easier to manage. Carefully, he guides us onto the bed so we're lying on our sides with him behind me. He brushes my hair from my face and kisses the back of my shoulder.

"So that's it?"

He chuckles against my shoulder blade. "Tell me how you really feel."

"No, I mean—" I struggle to find the words. "It's not so bad —the whole penis-swelling thing."

"It's called knotting," he corrects, playfully. "But I'm glad to hear it."

We settle into a comfortable silence, and as I listen to the sound of his breathing, I realize there's something we still need to say. "Hey Jamie."

"Yes, Raegan?" he answers sleepily.

"I love you."

He smiles against my back and pulls me tighter against him. "I love you, too."

Epilogue

"**W**hat do you think the chances are of me finding my mate if I walked into that camp right now?"

I give Joanna a once over from where I'm sitting in the passenger seat right as she parks her car in front of the entrance. She's wearing a T-shirt with a graphic of a chicken nugget dancing on a stripper pole.

"Take that shirt off, and I'd say it's pretty good."

We both whip our heads to the back seat where Jamie is texting absentmindedly.

"Don't say that!" I scold, playfully slapping his knee.

Joanna raises one eyebrow. "If he thinks it would work."

I scowl.

"Only because that shirt is ridiculous," he says. "No one will take you seriously."

Joanna *humphs*. "Nevermind."

Jamie shoves his phone into his pocket and leans forward to rest his chin on my shoulder. "Layton said his niece pretty much has the run of the place already."

At the end of the year, Jamie finally decided to hire

someone else to work full time at the coffee shop. He only goes in three days a week now, and it's given us plenty of extra time together.

To be honest, since Halloween, Jamie and I have spent way more time at home than anywhere else. It's been nice having the relationship to ourselves for a while, but by Thanksgiving it was time to make our relationship public.

Joanna was thrilled, Aidan was not surprised, and Kiki and Kendra both shrieked ecstatically when we told them, doing the job of letting the rest of the town know about the exciting news.

We've started going on walks around the neighborhood in the evenings, and we were able to introduce ourselves to the ghost family. Turns out they do eat cookies, so I made them several batches of chocolate chip. We've even had them over for dinner a couple of times! I asked about their dog, and they said they found him wandering around town and took him in.

I need to remember to tell Joanna to keep her eye open for any ghost animals without a home.

"She seemed to intimidate the shit out of Casey. Are they getting along?" I ask.

Jamie shrugs. "Casey's easy. They do whatever Layton and I say without a fuss. I don't think they'd give another manager a hard time."

"Yeah but, they looked extra scared when she came into her interview that day. More timid than usual."

Joanna rubs her hands together. "Ooo, is this a work drama? I wanna know?"

"It's not drama," Jamie retorts, shutting down her excitement. "Yet." He plants a kiss on my cheek and then pulls away to open the door and step outside into the cold winter night.

I crack the window. "Please stay warm," I plead to him through the inch wide space I've created. The harsh wind cuts across my cheeks. I hate the idea of him being out in the snow all night, but he's assured me, as always, that he'll be fine.

"Cuddle with the boys if you need to!" Joanna calls to him. Ever since learning about Jamie, Jo has developed a fascination with werewolves and pack relationships. She's also obsessed with the idea of finding her own mate.

I guess it would be fun for her to date one of Jamie's friends. I could see us going on double dates together. I've tried a few times to force Joanna and Aidan to be friendly, but they've held a bit of a grudge against one another since their first encounter. Jamie says they'll get over it, but I want them to get along, seeing as they're our two best friends.

Jamie rolls his eyes at Joanna's comment and blows me a kiss as he slides his index finger between the gap in the window to tap my nose. "Tell Cleetus to keep my spot warm until I get back."

I smile widely. At least those two are getting along. It took a month of side-eyes and empty threats, but Jamie eventually got used to my second favorite boy taking up space. Secretly, I think he's smitten. I totally caught them curled up peacefully together on the couch one night, but I kept it to myself.

I roll up the window and watch Jamie jog off toward camp. I spot Rhett waiting just inside the entrance wearing his new sheriff's uniform.

I guess the whole ordeal with Patrick and Banks was too much for Twitty Simmons, because after he found out I was almost stabbed in the middle of the Founding Day Festival, he stepped down as sheriff. He said the job was more than he signed up for. I guess his hopes of policing an idyllic small town were shattered when he realized there was actually crime to deal with. Personally, I think it's great that we have a werewolf in a position of power in Shadow Hills. It's about time things changed a little, and I know Rhett will be great at the job.

He handled everything with Banks way better than I thought. After an unsuccessful attempt to see eye to eye, Rhett ended up exiling him from the pack. He and Patrick picked up and moved to Florida. When I found out, my only reaction was 'good riddance!'

"Let's get out of here. I need sustenance." Jo turns out of the drive and back onto the road.

Since reconnecting, we make it a point to get together once a week and have girl time. And on the night's when Jamie has to shift, she comes over for a sleepover. Our friendship has become just as important to me as mine and Jamie's, and it's been nice having someone else to talk to about 'womanly things', as Jamie refers to it.

It's taken some time, but I think we've all finally reached a new semblance of normal. Jamie even decided to register himself legally as a werewolf, but we both were surprised to find he'd already been registered. His mother did it on his behalf the first day they moved here, and secretly, I think she didn't tell him because she wanted to give him time to accept what he is on his own terms.

We've both learned more about ourselves and grown thanks to what happened. I feel more confident and secure in my choices, and Jamie seems to feel truly happy embracing his wolf. It's brought us even closer together, and as hard as it was, I couldn't imagine things happening any other way.

Jamie and Raegan's story might be concluded, but you will see them again in the next *Monster Boyfriends* book, *HUNT: A Small Town Vampire Romance!*

Acknowledgments

This book was something I really needed for my own mental health. As much as I believe I was meant to write *Of Magic and Men*, it took a toll on me. I had to take time away from creating a unique world and just have some fun. *HOWL* reminded me why I love writing in the first place. It brought the joy back, and I seriously needed reminding!

First, let me thank my editor, Kelly! I'm so happy I was pointed in your direction, and I can't wait to work on future Monster Boyfriend books together!

Thank you Maria for designing another fantastic cover!

Thank you Olivia for lending me your talent and drawing my chapter headers and the art featured on each section intro! You've been a great friend over the years, and I'm so excited for you to start sharing your amazing art with more authors in the future!

Thank you to all the artists I've commissioned who made art for *HOWL*: Xena Fay, irdeinfierno, Indigo, and Elizabeth!

Thank you to everyone in the Author Support Group chat for answering questions and leading expertise to one another. I'm so grateful to have been welcomed into a group of women who are so open and happy to share what they've learned about this wild and crazy career we've all chosen!

Thank you to my bestie Yohannah for being my assistant at events and my constant cheerleader! You're my real life Jo <3

Thank you to my fur baby, Cleetus, for being perfect.

You're always there for me when I need you. I love your cuddles, and I hope all readers get a glimpse at how much you mean to me by reading about your likeness in this story.

Thank you to my husband for being my other half. My best friend and the love of my life. My Jamie.

Lastly, thank you to anyone who gave this book a chance. You are why I keep writing!

About the Author

Meg Alivien was born in Nashville, TN and currently resides outside the city with her husband and four cats! She loves binging her favorite tv shows (she deeply appreciates comedy horror with lots of blood), listening to audiobooks, and learning new recipes. Her favorite book genres are romance, mystery/thrillers, and fantasy!

facebook.com/authormegalivien

instagram.com/authormegalivien

threads.net/@authormegalivien

tiktok.com/@authormegalivien